ALWAYS A LAWMAN

USA TODAY Bestselling Author

DELORES FOSSEN

H HARLEQUIN INTRIGUE®

Recycling programs
for this product may
not exist in your area.

ISBN-13: 978-1-335-72137-2

Always a Lawman

Printed in U.S.A.

www.Harlequin.com

"Nearly ten years. I've waited long enough to finish what I started on the Blue River Ranch. This time, no one will be there to save you. This time, you will die."

Gabriel cursed. "You got this message, and you still came here?"

Jodi shrugged, tried to make it seem as if this didn't have her in knots.

"This proves my father's innocent," she said.

"No. A copycat could have written it. Or your father could have paid someone to do it."

"But I have to believe it wasn't a copycat. It's either that or accept that my father murdered both of your parents, attacked me and then left me for dead." She paused, shook her head. "Of course, no one in your family had trouble believing it."

"Neither did a jury," Gabriel pointed out.

"My father was convicted on circumstantial evidence," Jodi said, though she was preaching to the choir. Because as the sheriff and the son of the murdered couple, Gabriel knew the case better than everyone else.

Everyone but the real killer, that was.

Delores Fossen, a *USA TODAY* bestselling author, has sold over fifty novels with millions of copies of her books in print worldwide. She's received a Booksellers' Best Award and an RT Reviewers' Choice Best Book Award. She was also a finalist for a prestigious RITA® Award. You can contact the author through her website at www.deloresfossen.com.

Books by Delores Fossen

Harlequin Intrigue

Blue River Ranch

Always a Lawman

The Lawmen of Silver Creek Ranch

Grayson
Dade
Nate
Kade
Gage
Mason
Josh
Sawyer
Landon
Holden

HQN Books

The McCord Brothers

What Happens on the Ranch
(ebook novella)
Texas on My Mind
Cowboy Trouble
(ebook novella)
Lone Star Nights
Cowboy Underneath It All
(ebook novella)
Blame It on the Cowboy

A Wrangler's Creek Novel

Lone Star Cowboy
(ebook novella)
Those Texas Nights
One Good Cowboy
(ebook novella)
No Getting Over a Cowboy
Just Like a Cowboy
(ebook novella)
Branded as Trouble

Visit the Author Profile page at Harlequin.com for more titles.

CAST OF CHARACTERS

Sheriff Gabriel Beckett—On the tenth anniversary of his parents' brutal murders, Gabriel is not only getting death threats, but he also must protect his former flame, Jodi Canton, who's trying to use herself as bait to draw out a killer.

Jodi Canton—Ten years ago she was attacked and left for dead. Now there's a new threat, and she must turn to Gabriel even if she's not sure she wants the hot cowboy cop back in her life.

Travis Canton—Jodi's father is in jail for murdering Gabriel's parents, but even he's not sure if he committed the crimes.

August Canton—Jodi's uncle, who believes her father is innocent and that Jodi hasn't done enough to clear his name. He might be killing to cast doubt on Travis's murder convictions.

Billy Coleman—A troubled young man who could be a copycat killer, but his delicate mental state makes it hard to get answers from him.

Hector March—Head of the private security company where Jodi works. After Jodi's attack, he helped her get back on her feet, but he could have ulterior motives.

Russell Laney—Ten years ago, Jodi ended a relationship with him just days before she was attacked. Now Russell's getting death threats as well, but is he faking them to throw suspicion off himself?

Chapter One

She had died here. Temporarily, anyway.

But she was alive now, and Jodi Canton could feel the nerves just beneath the surface of her skin. With the Smith & Wesson gripped in her hand, she inched closer to the dump site where *he* had left her for dead.

There were no signs of the site now. Nearly ten years had passed, and the thick Texas woods had reclaimed the ground. It didn't look nearly so sinister dotted with wildflowers and a honeysuckle vine coiling over it. No drag marks.

No blood.

The years had washed it all away, but Jodi could see it, smell it and even taste it as if it were that sweltering July night when a killer had come within a breath of ending her life.

The nearby house had succumbed to time and the elements, too. It'd been a home then. Now, the white paint was blistered, and several of the windows on the bottom floor were closed off with boards that had grayed with age. Of course, she hadn't expected this place to ever feel like anything but the crime scene that it had once been.

Considering that two people had been murdered inside.

Jodi adjusted the grip on the gun when she heard the footsteps. They weren't hurried, but her visitor wasn't trying to sneak up on her, either. Jodi had been listening for that. Listening for everything that could get her killed.

Permanently this time.

Just in case she was wrong about who this might be, Jodi pivoted and took aim at him.

"You shouldn't have come here," he said. His voice was husky and deep, part lawman's growl, part Texas drawl.

The man was exactly who she thought it might be. Sheriff Gabriel Beckett. No surprise that he had arrived since this was Beckett land, and she'd parked in plain sight on the side of the road that led to the house. Even though the Becketts no longer lived here, Gabriel would have likely used the road to get to his current house.

"*You* came," Jodi answered, and she lowered her gun.

Muttering some profanity with that husky drawl, Gabriel walked to her side, his attention on the same area where hers was fixed. Or at least it was until he looked at her the same exact moment that she looked at him.

Their gazes connected.

And now it was Jodi who wanted to curse. *Really?* After all this time that punch of attraction was still there? She had huge reasons for the attraction to go away and not a single reason for it to stay.

Yet it remained.

At least on her part anyway. That wasn't heat she saw in Gabriel's eyes. Not attraction heat anyway. He was riled to the bone that she was back at the scene of the crime.

Gabriel hadn't changed much over the years. He was as lanky as he had been a decade ago. His dark brown hair was shorter now, but he still had those sizzling blue eyes. Still had the face that could make most women do a triple take. Simply put, he was one hot cowboy cop.

"Is it true?" Gabriel asked. "Are you actually remembering more details from the night of the attack?"

She'd expected the question and heard the skepticism in his voice. Skepticism that she deserved. Because her remembering anything else was a lie. "No. I told the press that because I thought it would draw out the real killer."

He gave her a look that could have frozen the hottest parts of hell. "That's not only stupid, it's dangerous. You made yourself a target."

"I'm already a target," she mumbled under her breath. And because she thought they needed a change of subject, Jodi tipped her head to the house. "I'm surprised it's still standing. Why haven't you bull-dozed it?"

A muscle tightened in his jaw. "There's a difference of opinion about that in the family."

Yes, Jodi had heard about some of those *opinions*. One of his sisters had wanted the place to remain standing, though Jodi had no idea why. She couldn't imagine any of them wanting to live in the house again. Still, maybe it was hard to demolish a childhood home even when that place was now a reminder of the nightmare.

"It's not a good time to be out here," he growled as if delivering an order that she would jump to obey. "And not just because you put out that lie to the press."

Jodi stayed put, and she darn sure didn't jump. "I was hoping if I saw the place again, it actually would help me remember, that what I told the press would no longer be a lie."

He aimed a scowl at her. Then, another scowl at the house and the spot where he'd found her bleeding and dying nearly a decade ago. "Why the heck would you want to remember that?"

He had a point. But so did Jodi. It wasn't a point that would likely make sense to Gabriel.

"I want to see his face." She shook her head. "I want to *remember* his face."

Ironically, it was one of the few things about that night that she couldn't recall. That particular detail was lost in the tangle of memories in her head. She could feel the slice of the knife as it cut into her body.

The pain.

Jodi could remember the blood draining from her. But she couldn't see the man who'd been responsible for turning her life on a dime.

"Why come back now?" Gabriel demanded. "Why tell the press that you're remembering after all this time?"

Good questions. And she had good answers.

"I got an email." Jodi figured that would get his attention, and it did.

Gabriel turned those lethal blue eyes on her. "What kind of email?"

She took out the printed copy from the front pocket of her jeans and handed it to him. Jodi didn't need to see what was written there. She'd memorized every word.

Nearly ten years. I've waited long enough to finish what I started on the Blue River Ranch. This time, no one will be there to save you. This time, you will die.

Gabriel cursed again. "You got this, and you still came here?"

Jodi shrugged, tried to make it seem as if this message didn't have her in knots. It did. But then, she'd been in knots for a long time now. For ten painful years. In some sick way, maybe this meant there'd be a showdown, and the knots would finally loosen.

"This proves my father's innocent," she said and waited for Gabriel to blast that to smithereens.

It didn't take long before he attempted that blast. "No. A copycat could have written it. Or your father could have paid someone to do it."

Both could be true, and she acknowledged that with a slight sound of agreement. "But I have to believe it wasn't a copycat. It's either that or accept that my father murdered both of your parents, attacked me and then left me for dead." She paused, shook her head. "Of course, no one in your family had trouble believing it."

"Neither did a jury," Gabriel pointed out.

It was true. A jury had indeed convicted her father, Travis, of two counts of murder and also of her own attack, and the jurors had given him two consecutive life sentences without the possibility of parole. He was rotting away in a jail cell, exactly where the Becketts wanted him. Of course, it could have been worse. Travis could have gotten the death penalty, but thankfully the DA had backed off on that because of some weaknesses in the case.

No eye witness to put Travis at the scene, and

the fact that her father couldn't recall what'd gone on that night.

"My father was convicted on circumstantial evidence," Jodi said, though she was preaching to the choir. Because as the sheriff and the son of the murdered couple, Gabriel knew the case better than everyone else.

Everyone but the real killer, that is.

"My father didn't have the murder weapon on him when the cops found him," she went on. Yes, Gabriel knew that, too, but she wanted to remind him. "And the wounds to your parents and to me were made with a unique knife."

"A skinning knife with a crescent-shaped blade. Is this going somewhere?" he continued without hesitating. "Because it doesn't matter that your father claimed he didn't own a knife like that—"

"He didn't," she interrupted. "I was the one who cleaned the house. Cleaned his room. The barn. You name it, I cleaned it, and I never saw a blade that resembled anything like a crescent."

It wasn't easy for her to talk about the knife. But even when she didn't talk about it, the image of it was still clear in her head. Not from that night, though. Jodi hadn't actually seen it, but the FBI had shown her photos of a skinning knife. And they were certain that's what had been used on her because the tip of it had broken off during the attack. The surgeon had removed it from what'd been left of her spleen.

"That doesn't mean Travis didn't have that knife hidden away," Gabriel countered. "And I don't care if he says he didn't. Nor do I care that he claims he can't remember anything from that night because he had three times more than the legal limit of alcohol. The bottom line is that he had motive, and my father's blood on his shirt."

Blood that someone could have planted there when Travis was passed out drunk by the Blue River, where the deputies had found him hours after the murders and her own attack.

Jodi couldn't have argued that her alcoholic father hadn't been in any shape to murder two people, one of them sheriff at the time. That's because the DA had successfully argued that Travis could have gotten drunk afterward.

And yes, her father did have motive.

Bad blood between him and the Becketts. Feuds over land and water rights that had been going on before Jodi was born. It had created the perfect trifecta for law enforcement. Her father had had the means, motive and opportunity to butcher two people and then turn that knife on Jodi when he thought maybe she'd witnessed what he had done.

She hadn't.

Because of the blasted tears she'd been crying over Gabriel's rejection, she hadn't seen anything. She'd barely had time to hear the footsteps before her attacker had clubbed her on the head and started stabbing her.

"Have you considered the reason you don't remember your attacker's face is because you blocked it out?" Gabriel asked a moment later. "Because it was too traumatic for you to see the face of the man that you thought loved you?"

Jodi had to take a moment to try to tamp down the panic rising inside her. No way could she believe that.

"My father never confessed to the murders," she pointed out.

"That doesn't mean he didn't do it," he countered and then huffed. No doubt signaling an end to an argument they'd been having for a decade. He looked at the email again. "You gave a copy of this to the FBI?"

She nodded, annoyed that it was a question. "Of course I gave it to them since they're the ones who handled this investigation. With you and your brother's help, of course."

In fact, Gabriel's brother, Jameson, had pretty much spearheaded the case in the beginning. Not that anyone had been dragging their feet. No. Everyone seemed to be racing toward any evidence that would result in her father's conviction. But Jameson had been a key player in getting that guilty verdict.

"I just wanted to make sure you didn't withhold anything from the FBI," Gabriel added. "Because they need to see any and all threats, so they can put a stop to them."

Jodi's annoyance went up a notch. Gabriel was talking down to her. Talking to her as if she was a criminal. Or an idiot. "I know you don't think much of what I do for a living, but I'd have no reason to keep something like that to myself."

He handed her back the email, his gaze connecting with hers again, and she got another dose of his doubt.

Gabriel definitely didn't think much of what she did. Consultant for Sentry, a private security firm. Many cops thought that Sentry toed the line when it came to investigations.

And sometimes they did.

"I don't wear one of these," she said, tapping his badge, "but that doesn't mean I'm not out for justice just like you, Jameson and your deputies."

"Justice at any price," he argued.

She shrugged, trying to make sure she didn't look as if that'd stung a little. "Repeating my boss's motto—the law isn't always justice."

"Hector March." Gabriel said her boss's name as if it were profanity. To him, it was. "Is he out of jail yet?"

That was another jab. And another sting. "Yes. And for the record, what Hector did was definitely justice. The illegal video surveillance he set up eventually led to the arrest of a pimp who was known for beating up his girls. He used his fists to do whatever he wanted, and now he's been stopped."

There was too much emotion in her voice now. Too much emotion inside her, as well. It was hard to rein in the feelings of being powerless against a much stronger attacker, but Jodi had had a lot of practice doing just that.

"The pimp would have gone to jail eventually through legal means," Gabriel growled.

It was probably the truth. Probably. But Hector had made it happen a little sooner than the cops could have managed it.

"If I can save one woman from getting beaten or killed, I'll do it," Jodi insisted. "And yes, I'm overidentifying."

She waved off any other part of this discussion that might happen because she'd admitted that. It was obvious Gabriel and she were never going to agree when it came to Sentry, Hector or her job. Jodi also didn't want to keep talking about something that couldn't change. She'd nearly died. Had the scars to prove it. Nothing was going to undo that.

"You blame me for what happened to you." Gabriel threw that out there like a gauntlet.

She turned toward him so fast that her neck popped. Jodi wanted to say no, that she didn't. Better yet, she wanted to believe it. But she didn't. Not completely anyway.

"I know in here it wasn't your fault." She touched

her fingers to her head. "But everything that happened that night has gotten all rolled into one tangled mess inside me. A mess that involves you, me…and the killer. I don't want to include you in that nightmare, but it did begin with you, and I can't just forget that."

"Yeah," he said and looked away. Gabriel always looked away whenever the subject of attraction or sex came up between them. And despite her near murder not actually being about sex, it was sex that had started it all.

Or rather, lack of sex.

"You were nineteen," he reminded her. "Too young to be with me."

Obviously, his mind had hitched a ride on the exact train of thought as hers. "I was an adult."

"Barely. You were also one of my kid sister's best friends. And I was five years older than you. There's a world of difference between a nineteen-year-old college student and a twenty-four-year-old deputy sheriff. Legally, you weren't jailbait, but that still didn't make being with you right."

It was his old argument that she knew all too well since it was the same one he'd used the night of the attack. She'd been staying in the Beckett house, a guest of Gabriel's sister Ivy, who at the time was also her college roommate. Around 10:00 p.m., Jodi had walked the less than a quarter of a mile distance between the Becketts' and Gabriel's place, the house left to him by his grandparents. And Jodi had done that for the sole purpose of seducing Gabriel.

It hadn't worked.

"You turned me down," she said under her breath. Thankfully, it didn't sound as if she still carried a decade of hurt. But it had certainly hurt then. Simply put, Gabriel Beckett was the only man she'd ever wanted. It was ironic, though, that after the night of the attack she'd never wanted him or another man again.

She silently cursed. That was a partial lie. A lie she could feel now that she was standing so close to Gabriel. Much to her disgust, she still wanted him.

"Sex is a commitment," she mumbled. "That's what you told me when you turned me away," Jodi huffed. "Which wasn't the truth since you had sex with half the women in town, and you didn't *commit* to any of them."

He said something under his breath that she didn't catch. Then, something she did catch. Bad profanity. "Why did you really come here? Because I'm not buying it that you're here just to remember. Are you trying to draw out the person who sent you the email?"

She didn't deny it. Jodi did indeed want to draw him out in the open and put an end to this once and for all.

"He could just shoot you," Gabriel reminded her.

"I don't think so. I think he wants his hands on me

again." Just saying it nearly made her gag. "I won't be the victim for the rest of my life."

"Then start by not being here." Gabriel paused and glanced around. The kind of glance that a lawman made as if checking to make sure no one else was there. "You're not the only one who got a threatening email."

Everything inside her went still. "Who else? *You?*"

Gabriel nodded. "All three of my siblings, too. Jameson, Ivy and Lauren."

Jodi hadn't needed their names. She'd grown up next to the Becketts and knew them well enough to know their birthdays. Now, of course, they were her enemies. Enemies who'd apparently gotten death threats.

"What'd the emails say?" she asked.

Gabriel drew in a weary breath. "Almost the same as yours. Except for mine. The threat was, well, more explicit. Probably because I'm the sheriff now."

Jodi tried to process that. "What possible reason would my father have to send threats like this?"

"I've given up trying to figure out why killers do what they do." He hesitated again. "But I'm leaning more toward a copycat. There are a lot of sick people out there, and the story got plenty of press. With the tenth anniversary coming up in three months, I believe it's bringing out the lunatics."

"So, you think the emails are empty threats?" Jodi

hated to sound disappointed. Hated even more that she was disappointed that it might be true. It sickened her to think the truth had already played out.

And that her father had left her for dead.

"Copycat threats aren't always empty," Gabriel corrected. "That's why I don't want you out here. Not alone anyway. If you want to try to jog your memory again, call me, and I'll have someone meet you."

Jodi probably should be insulted because she was an expert marksman and trained in hand-to-hand combat. She could protect herself.

Probably.

And it was the fact that the *probably* was not a certainty that kept her up at night.

She turned, ready to head back to her car, but something caught her eye. Some movement in one of the second-floor windows. Gabriel must have seen it, too, because he stepped in front of her.

And he drew his gun.

Jodi pulled her weapon, too. "Should there be anyone in the house?" she asked.

"No." That time he absolutely didn't hesitate, and Gabriel started toward the porch. "Before you jump to conclusions, it's probably just a teenager out for a stupid thrill. Or maybe a reporter. Either way, you should go to your car now."

"Just in case it turns out to be something more than a teen or a reporter, I can back you up if you're going inside."

Which he apparently was.

Gabriel didn't turn down her offer of backup. Didn't order her to her car again, either. Maybe because he figured she could be attacked while heading to the road. It was obvious he was thinking this was more than just a false alarm. Of course, after those threatening emails, Jodi doubted there was anything false about it, either.

Mercy. Was the killer here?

That sent her heartbeat racing, the sound of it throbbing in her ears. The memories came. Too many of them too fast. She had to force them back into that little box she'd built in her mind. This was no time for a panic attack. Not in front of a killer.

Not in front of Gabriel, either.

He took slow, cautious steps, his gaze firing not just to the window but all around them. "I'm Sheriff Gabriel Beckett," he called out. "You're trespassing. Come out with your hands in the air."

Nothing.

It was hard to hear because of her racing pulse and the breeze rattling through the live oaks, but Jodi thought she heard someone moving around inside. There were plenty of windows on the back part of the house that the intruder could use to escape. But maybe he didn't have escape in mind.

Maybe this would turn into another attempt to murder her.

If so, she was ready.

"Stay behind me," Gabriel insisted. "And watch our backs."

She did, and Jodi continued to keep an eye out as they made their way up the steps to the porch. But as soon as Gabriel reached the top step, he stopped.

Then, he froze.

Jodi was near enough to him to sense the muscles tensing in his body. And she soon realized why.

Her heart jumped to her throat. "Oh, mercy." Jodi shook her head and inched closer. Not that she needed to be closer to realize what she was seeing.

A knife.

With a crescent-shaped blade. The tip was missing.

And there was blood on it.

Chapter Two

Even before he saw the knife. Gabriel had already had a bad feeling. He'd gotten it the moment he laid eyes on Jodi because she should be nowhere near this place. Now, that bad feeling turned to something much worse.

Hell.

Just to be sure his eyes weren't playing tricks on him, he took another look at what someone had left on the porch just about two feet to the left side of the door. No tricks. It was the knife all right. Or rather, *a* knife.

"That blood on it isn't dry," Jodi pointed out. Her voice was trembling just a little, but Gabriel had to hand it to her because she was holding herself together.

On the outside anyway.

On the inside, he figured it was a whole different story. If it was indeed the knife that had killed his parents, then it was the same one the killer had used on Jodi.

"It could be fake blood," Gabriel reminded her.

There was no way he would touch it to find out, though. Since the tip was missing, this was either the actual weapon that had killed his parents or else someone had broken off the end of the blade so that it would resemble it.

But there was a problem with that.

The missing tip that the surgeon had removed from Jodi's body hadn't been mentioned in any of the police reports. Nor was the fact that the killer had taken his father's watch and his mother's necklace. Those were just a few of the little details that the FBI had left out in case some nutjob tried to confess to the crime. So, either someone had hacked into those actual reports, or...

Gabriel didn't want to speculate about an *or* just yet.

While keeping his attention on their surroundings, Gabriel took his phone from his pocket and texted Jameson. He told him that he needed his help and for him to call a CSI to come and take custody of this knife. Jameson was at his house and could be there in a couple of minutes.

Bringing in his brother was better than waiting for the deputies to come in from the sheriff's office. Besides, Jameson was a Texas Ranger and the best backup Gabriel could have. Once Jameson arrived, maybe they could keep Jodi out of this. Of course, the problem was that she was here and therefore already in the middle of it.

Whatever *it* was.

This could still be a prank, and Gabriel was holding on to that hope. Over the years the house had become a magnet for daredevil kids, ghost hunters and pretty much anyone warped enough to want to see an old crime scene. That's how the windows had gotten broken and the boards sprayed with graffiti.

Gabriel tested the doorknob. Locked, just as it should be, and he used his key to open it. He pushed open the door, had a look around and got an instant punch of the musty smell and the dust. An instant punch of the memories, too.

He hated this place.

Hated that it still felt like an open, raw wound. A cut so deep that it would never heal. It was no doubt the same for Jodi. Even though she hadn't lost her parents that day, it had been just as costly for her.

In plenty of ways, she'd lost herself.

For just a moment he got a flash of another memory. Of the smiling nineteen-year-old who'd shown up at his house that night. She'd been wearing cut-off denim shorts, a snug red top and had looked far better than a girl had a right to look.

He pushed that memory aside, too. He'd lost himself that night, as well. Because he hadn't protected her. He hadn't saved his parents, and while Jodi had lived, he darn sure hadn't saved her, either.

Gabriel didn't see anyone in either of the two rooms just off the entry. Nor did he hear anyone. He ducked under the crisscross of boards, his back scraping against the rough wood. He moved just far enough inside for Jodi to step in behind him. Even though she didn't say anything, he could hear her breathing. Which was too fast.

There were no signs of an intruder here. No footprints in the dust on the hardwood floors.

The furniture in the living and dining rooms was still draped with the sheets that his sisters had put on them years earlier. It hadn't felt right to move anything after the CSIs had finished with it, so they'd covered everything, locked and boarded it up. Now, it was like some kind of sick time capsule.

"Anyone up there?" Gabriel called out.

He didn't expect a response and didn't get one. But what he did hear was something he didn't want to hear.

A footstep.

Yeah, someone was definitely upstairs. And judging from the weight of the step, it wasn't a raccoon or some other animal.

Jodi moved as if ready to barge right up there, but Gabriel leaned in front of her and shot her a scowl. "We'll wait here for Jameson. Once he arrives, I'll go upstairs. Alone."

She huffed, clearly not pleased about that. Maybe because she wanted to confront the person who'd left the knife. Of course, she thought it was the same person who had attacked her, but Gabriel was sticking to his guns that her father had been responsible for that.

"We should at least check the back door," she suggested. "That might be how he got in."

Yes, either that or a window. The place wasn't exactly a fortress, though the doors and windows should have at least all been locked. That wouldn't have stopped someone from breaking one of the panes and getting inside, though.

Gabriel went to the center of the foyer, and he volleyed his attention around the rooms and the stairs. He still didn't see anyone or anything out of place. Definitely no more blood to go along with what was on that knife, and if he had seen so much as a drop, he would have stopped and gotten out of there since this could potentially be a crime scene.

Again.

But thankfully there was nothing other than the bad feeling that continued to snake down his spine.

"Stay here," he warned Jodi.

Whether she would or not was anyone's guess, but Gabriel went into the adjacent family room so he could peer through to the kitchen. No one was there, but the rear door was open. The wind was causing it to sway just enough to make this whole ordeal even creepier than it already was.

Gabriel was about to lose patience with himself and whoever the hell had broken in, and he probably would have just charged upstairs if he hadn't heard a sound that he actually wanted to hear.

"What the hell?" someone asked and then added a string of profanity.

Jameson.

He'd probably seen the knife. Or maybe the cussing was for Jodi. Not that Jameson had anything in particular against Jodi, but he would have known it wasn't a good idea for her to be here.

"Someone's upstairs," Jodi said to his brother.

With his gun already drawn, Jameson came into the house, stepping around her, and his attention went straight to Gabriel. "Did the intruder leave the knife?"

"I'm not sure." But Gabriel was about to find out. "Stay here with Jodi."

"The CSIs are on the way," Jameson told him as Gabriel started up the stairs. "I called Cameron, too."

Cameron Doran. A deputy and family friend. Cameron would have been at his own house on the ranch grounds, and while Gabriel appreciated the double backup, he hoped it wouldn't be necessary.

With his gun aimed, Gabriel went up the stairs, pausing after each step to listen for any footsteps or movement. He didn't hear anything other than that damn creaky door downstairs.

At first anyway.

Then, there were definitely footsteps, and they appeared to be coming from his parents' bedroom. No more pausing for him. Gabriel hurried up the stairs and to the landing so he could pivot in that direction.

No one was in the hall, so he went toward the bedroom, passing several others along the way. He kept watch around him. The doors were all closed, but that didn't mean someone wouldn't open one of them and start shooting. Or running anyway. He was still hoping this would turn out to be nothing.

By the time Gabriel made it the forty or so feet to his parents' room, he'd worked up a sweat. And it wasn't helping his temper. This was not how he wanted to spend his afternoon.

He kicked open the door, and he nearly fired when he saw the movement. But it was just the white gauzy curtains fluttering in the breeze.

"He's out back, and he's getting away!" Jodi shouted.

Hell.

Gabriel hurried to the window to look out, and the first thing he spotted was the ladder propped up against the back of the house. But there were no signs of the person who'd put it there.

However, there were signs of Jodi and Jameson.

He saw them run into the yard, such that it was. Once it'd been a manicured lawn, but now it was overgrown with weeds and underbrush.

"Stop or I'll shoot," Jameson called out.

Gabriel saw the guy then. He was dressed all in black, like some kind of ninja, and he was running into the woods. There were plenty of places to hide there and even some old ranch trails where the guy could have stashed a vehicle. Gabriel wanted to stop him because he had some answering to do about that knife.

Jameson and Jodi went after him, and that sent Gabriel hurrying, as well. He didn't go down the ladder because that would have made him an easy target in case the intruder was armed. Instead, he barreled down the hall and stairs and hurried out the back door.

Jameson and Jodi had gotten way ahead of him by now and had disappeared into the woods. With any luck, they were on the intruder's heels. Well, hopefully Jameson was. Gabriel didn't like it that a civilian was in the mix of things. Especially *this* civilian. Despite Jodi's attempt at trying to keep her composure when she saw the knife, Gabriel knew it caused her to have a slam of bad memories.

Once he was in the backyard, he had to hurdle over some of the underbrush, and it took him several long moments of hard running before he spotted Jameson and Jodi again. He'd hardly gotten a glimpse of them before Gabriel heard something else that caused his heart to jump into overdrive.

A cracking sound.

A shot being fired through a silencer.

Gabriel cursed again because neither Jodi's nor Jameson's guns were rigged that way. That meant the shot had come from the intruder. Well, that blew his theory that this was all some kind of sick prank. If the idiot had come here armed, then he meant business.

But what kind of business exactly?

If he'd wanted to kill them, he could have done that when Jodi and he had been talking earlier.

Jameson and Jodi thankfully ducked behind some trees, and using massive oaks as cover, Gabriel darted behind them as he made his way to Jodi. Jameson was only several yards away, and both of them had their guns and attention directed at a thick cluster of bushes and weeds.

Jodi was breathing through her mouth, but other than that, she was holding it together. And she looked like the trained security specialist that she was.

"Did you get a look at his face?" Gabriel wanted to know.

She shook her head and spared him a glance. Gabriel saw it then. The fear. But he also saw the determination to get her hands on this guy.

"Do you see him?" Jameson asked.

Gabriel peered around the tree for a glance. But he didn't get much of a look. That's because a bullet smacked into the bark just inches from his head. A second shot quickly followed.

He cursed and pulled Jodi to the ground. Gabriel hadn't intended to land on her, but that's what happened. The front of his body right on her back. They'd never been lovers, but being pressed against her gave Gabriel a jolt of attraction. A jolt he quickly shoved aside so he could adjust his position in case he got a chance to return fire.

The intruder fired again, and Gabriel tried to pinpoint the shot. Hard to do with the silencer, but he was pretty sure he knew the guy's general area.

"Stop shooting and come out with your hands up," Gabriel shouted out to him.

He didn't expect the intruder to do that.

And was stunned when he did.

"I'm coming out," the man said.

Jodi went stiff and practically shoved Gabriel off her so that she could get to her feet. Gabriel did the same, and he muscled her behind him just in case this was some kind of trick.

But it wasn't.

The man stood, his hands raised in the air. In addition to the black clothes, he was also wearing a ski mask and gloves.

"Where's your gun?" Gabriel snapped.

"On the ground near my feet."

Gabriel didn't want it anywhere near this fool. "Walk toward us. Slowly. Don't make any sudden moves, and remember that part about keeping your hands in the air."

The guy gave a shaky nod, and he started toward

them. Jameson came out from cover, his gun trained on the guy. Gabriel and Jodi did the same, and the moment he was close enough to Jameson, his brother hurried to the man, put him facedown on the ground and frisked him.

"Keep watch around us," Gabriel told Jodi.

Her eyes widened a moment, and she must have realized that this man might have brought a *friend* or two with him.

Gabriel went closer to the guy, too, and handed Jameson a pair of plastic cuffs that he took from his pocket. Jameson immediately put them on him.

"Who the hell are you?" Gabriel asked the man.

Gabriel stooped down and yanked off the ski mask. His head was shaved, and there were several homemade tattoos on his forehead and neck. Definitely not someone Gabriel recognized, and judging from the way Jameson shook his head, neither did his brother.

"I'm not saying nothing until I talk to my lawyer," the guy answered. He sounded pretty defiant for someone who'd just surrendered.

But Jodi had some defiance of her own. She got right in the guy's face. "Where did you get that knife?"

He smiled. A sick kind of smile that had Gabriel's insides twisting. He wasn't sure what the heck this was all about, but he intended to find out.

"I'll take him to the sheriff's office," Gabriel said. "He can call his lawyer, and I'll question him." Then, he turned to the guy and hoped he could change his mind about clamming up. "Just so you know, you're looking at three counts of attempted murder."

The guy smiled again. Gabriel sure didn't. He silently cursed. Because they could be dealing with someone who was mentally unstable. If so, they might never get answers. But Jodi clearly wasn't giving up on that just yet.

She was right at the goon's side as Jameson started leading him back to the house. "Tell me where you got the knife."

Gabriel doubted the guy was about to blurt out anything, but just in case, he went ahead and read him his rights. Jodi waited, the impatience all over her face, and the moment Gabriel finished, she repeated her demand.

Nothing. Well, she got nothing other than the smile that Gabriel wished he could knock off the idiot's face.

"He's too young to have been part of your attack," Gabriel reminded Jodi. This guy was barely twenty, maybe still in his teens. He would have been just a kid a decade ago.

"He could still know something about it," she pointed out just as quickly.

"Yeah," Gabriel admitted. "That's why I'll handle this. You should go home, and I'll let you know if he says anything."

That earned him a glare. He'd expected it. She

wasn't about to back away from this, but Gabriel had
to keep her at bay because he didn't want her compromising his investigation.

"Need some help?" someone called out.

Cameron. The deputy was hurrying around the
side of the house toward them. He, too, had his weapon
drawn.

"Did you come here in your cruiser?" Gabriel
asked him.

Cameron nodded. "Who is this guy? And why is
the knife on the porch?"

Good questions. "I'm hoping he'll tell me once
we've booked him." Gabriel tipped his head to the
woods. "This clown left a gun out there. Keep an eye
on it until the CSIs get here to collect it, and then
I'll need Jameson and you to drive him to the sheriff's office. I'll be right behind you as soon as I've
talked to the CSIs."

And after he'd had a look around.

Something more than the obvious wasn't right.

Jameson headed to the cruiser with the prisoner,
and Cameron started for the woods. Jodi didn't
budge.

"I want to be there when you question him," she
insisted.

"No." And he wasn't going to compromise on that.
At best he would allow her to watch from the observation room, but Gabriel was sure even that wasn't
a good idea.

Gabriel looked at her, and that's when he saw that she was trembling. Jodi realized he'd noticed, too, and she cursed under her breath.

"I'm fine," she snapped. Her blond hair was damp with sweat, and she pushed it from her face. Her face was beaded with sweat, as well.

They stared at each other, until Jodi glanced away. "Sometimes, I have panic attacks," she said.

He figured she had to be close to one now to admit something like that. It didn't go well with her tough Sentry employee image.

"The water is still on in the house since it comes from a well. I wouldn't drink it because there might be rust in the pipes, but it might help if you splash some on your face."

But the moment he made the offer, it occurred to him why he still had that niggling feeling in his gut. Gabriel's attention zoomed to the back door.

"What?" Jodi asked when she followed his gaze.

"The ladder's there, but the back door was open when I went into the house."

She made a sound to indicate she was giving that some thought. "Well, the guy used the ladder to escape. Jameson and I saw him running from it when we got to the backyard."

Yeah. So, maybe the open back door had nothing to do with their perp. Still, Gabriel intended to check it out. When he'd run through the house to go in pursuit, he hadn't looked around to see if anything else had been...disturbed.

Gabriel started toward the porch with Jodi following along behind him. Part of him wanted to tell her to stay put while he checked it out, but it might not be safe for her to be out here alone. Of course, she would believe she could take care of herself, but if that idiot had indeed brought help, there could be more gunfire.

He didn't slow down until he reached the back door, and then Gabriel paused just to take in the room. The gray tile didn't show the dust, which meant it didn't show any footprints, either. That didn't mean some weren't there, though, so he used his elbow to open the door as wide as it would go, and he stepped to the side.

Jodi stayed in the doorway, but they seemed to spot something at the same time. She made a slight gasping sound.

Because the thing they spotted appeared to be drops of blood.

Gabriel reminded himself that it could be fake. Just like the blood on the knife. But that didn't stop the tightness in his chest.

"Come inside but stay back," he told her. He definitely didn't want her following what appeared to be a trail of blood drops. Drops that led right to the pantry.

The door to the pantry was ajar but not open

enough for Gabriel to see if there was anyone or anything inside. With his gun ready, he went closer, and behind him he could hear Jodi shifting her position, as well. No doubt getting ready in case they were about to be attacked again.

As soon as he was close enough, Gabriel gave the door a kick with the toe of his boot. He took aim.

Then he cursed.

Hell.

There was more blood here, pooled on the floor amid the toppled cans. And in the middle of all that blood was what appeared to be a dead body.

Chapter Three

Breathe.

Jodi kept repeating that reminder to herself.

She couldn't keep taking in those short bursts of air that could cause her to hyperventilate. She needed normal breaths because that was her best bet right now at staving off a panic attack.

Gabriel certainly wasn't doing anything to put her at ease. He was seated at his desk at the sheriff's office building on Main Street in Blue River, and he was on his umpteenth phone call since they'd arrived two hours earlier. Jameson and Cameron were in the squad room, and they were doing the same thing.

Obviously there was lots to do now that this was a murder investigation. In addition to the calls and fielding questions from his deputies, Gabriel also kept glancing up at her.

Not that he had to glance far.

Jodi was pacing across his office while she tried to keep herself together.

What Gabriel wasn't doing was questioning their suspect. The bald kid who'd fired shots at them. Maybe a kid who had committed the murder, too. And had also left the knife on the porch. But Gabriel wouldn't have a chance of confirming any of that until the kid's lawyer arrived. Whenever that would be.

Gabriel finally finished his latest call, and immediately started making some notes on his computer. "You should go home," he said. And since Jodi was the only other person in the room, that order was obviously meant for her. "I can have one of the reserve deputies drive you and stay with you until this is all sorted out."

"I'm staying here," she insisted.

Then, she huffed, a little insulted that Gabriel had thought she couldn't take care of herself and needed a deputy. His doubt about her abilities probably had to do with that look that kept crossing her face, the one indicating she was about to have a panic attack. Jodi hated that it was there. Hated that it felt as if she might lose it at any moment, but that wouldn't stop her from defending herself if someone came after her again.

"What did the ME have to say about the body?" she asked.

His eyebrow came up, maybe to show her that he was surprised that she'd known he was talking to the ME. She hadn't heard anything the ME said, but she had been able to tell from Gabriel's questions who'd been on the other end of the phone line.

"He's a white male in his mid- to late thirties," Gabriel answered after a short hesitation. "There was no ID on him. Cause of death appears to be exsanguination from multiple stab wounds to the torso."

Breathe.

That felt like a punch to the chest. Because just hearing the words caused the memories to come. Memories of her own blood loss from stab wounds.

Mercy.

She'd lost so much blood that night that her heart had stopped for a couple of seconds. The medics had brought her back, but it could have gone either way. She could have ended up like the dead man in the Becketts' house. Or like Gabriel's parents who had died on their kitchen floor.

"Is this never going to end?" Jodi said before she could stop herself.

Gabriel cursed, got up from his desk and took hold of her arm. Good thing, too, because she suddenly wasn't too steady on her feet. He put her in the chair and got her a bottle of water from the small fridge in the corner.

"This is why you shouldn't be here," he insisted. "This is too much for you."

"It's too much for all of us."

He certainly didn't argue with that, but he did sit on the armrest and stare down at her. She saw it all in his eyes. His own battle with the nightmarish memories. His unease at her being there.

Except it was more than unease.

Oh, no. It was that attraction again. Anytime they were within breathing distance of each other, the heat returned. Thankfully, they were both in a place to shove it away. It wouldn't stay gone. But for now, they could keep it at bay.

"How do you think he got the knife?" Jodi pressed.

Gabriel lifted his shoulder. "Maybe he found it. I would say it's a duplicate, but there's the problem with only a handful of people knowing about the broken tip. Of course, a handful is more than enough for the info to leak and get to the wrong person. If so, he could be just some nutjob copycat."

All of that made sense, but it didn't exactly soothe her raw nerves. Too bad Gabriel didn't have a theory that would clear her father's name.

Gabriel gave a heavy sigh. "Look, I don't know what happened, but if this guy confesses to sending the threatening emails and committing the murder, then maybe this will put an end to it." He added another shrug when she stared at him. "Well, for everyone but your father."

Yes. Her father would get a different kind of ending. This wouldn't do a thing to get Travis out of jail.

Jodi looked away from him at the exact moment she felt Gabriel's hand on her shoulder. She didn't jump out of her skin as she usually did from an unexpected touch. In fact, it felt far more comforting than it should.

And that's the reason she stood and moved away from him.

That got his attention. Something she hadn't particularly wanted to get right now. Gabriel was giving her the once-over with those lawman's eyes, and he was obviously waiting for an explanation.

"I just have trouble being touched sometimes," she settled for saying.

A lie. She had trouble with it *all the time*.

He drew his eyebrows together. "Uh, have you gotten help for it?"

She nodded. That wasn't a lie. She'd attempted to get help by seeing a string of therapists. "In my case, help didn't work."

He kept staring at her, clearly still wanting more. She'd already told him far more than she'd spilled to anyone else, and Jodi didn't want to get any deeper into it. He probably wouldn't understand that the only thing that eased the demons was the knowledge that she could now defend herself.

Thankfully, she didn't have to add more because there was movement in the doorway. Jodi automatically reached for her gun, but it was just Cameron.

Cameron had lawman's eyes, too, and he slid a glance between Gabriel and her. The corner of his mouth lifted a fraction and for just a second. A dimple flashed in his cheek.

"You two always did have a thing for each other," he drawled.

Heaven knew what Cameron had seen or sensed to make him say that or to make him give that half smile, but it caused Gabriel to scowl. Unlike most people, Cameron didn't seem to be affected by that particular expression from the king of scowls. Probably because he'd had a lifetime of scowls tossed at him. After all, Gabriel wasn't just his boss, but they'd been friends since childhood.

"Do you have a reason to be here?" Gabriel snapped.

Cameron gave them that lazy smile again, and he handed her a cup of coffee and a small white bag. "It's some doughnuts from the diner. Thought you might need a sugar fix right about now."

She wasn't hungry in the least. In fact, Jodi wasn't sure she'd be able to hold anything down, but Cameron's gesture touched her. "You remembered I have a sweet tooth," she said.

"Hard to forget it. I remember having to wrestle some chocolate cake away from you once when we were kids."

Jodi nodded. "And I had to wrestle them from Lauren and your sister, Gilly."

She caught the slight change in Cameron's expression and knew she'd hit a nerve. Two of them, actually. From what Jodi had heard, Gilly had died during childbirth, and Cameron was raising her child. Since that'd happened only a few months earlier, the grief still had to be raw.

However, there was another rawness, too. One that might never go away, as well. Once, Cameron had been in love with Lauren. And vice versa. But again, those feelings of young love had all been shattered the night of the murders because Cameron had been a deputy then, and Lauren had blamed him for not preventing her parents' deaths. It probably wasn't logical for Lauren to feel that way, but those sorts of raw feelings weren't always logical.

"Yes," Cameron said as if he knew what she was thinking.

His smile stayed in place a moment longer before his attention shifted to Gabriel. "The CSIs are processing the knife right away. We should know soon if the blood belongs to the victim and if there are prints that match our suspect.

"Sorry," Cameron added to Jodi. "This kind of talk doesn't exactly go well with coffee and doughnuts."

"It's all right. I want to know what's happening with the case. Has the kid said anything?" she asked. "Or has his lawyer arrived yet?"

Cameron shook his head to both of her questions. "Nothing from him, but you do have a visitor, and he's demanding to see you. It's your boss, Hector March."

Gabriel shot her a glance, one that seemed like

an accusation. "I didn't call him," Jodi insisted. And she looked to Cameron for answers. "The murder is already on the news?"

The deputy nodded.

Good grief. That hadn't taken long at all, but then, she hadn't expected it to stay quiet. Still, she hadn't wanted to deal with Hector when her nerves were this close to the surface.

Jodi stood, trying to steel herself up by taking some deep breaths and flexing her hands. "Where is he?"

Cameron hitched his thumb toward the squad room. "I had him wait out there. Something he's not very happy about. Apparently, he's not the waiting-around sort."

No, he wasn't. But if Jodi tried to put Hector off, that would only make him dig in his heels even more. She reminded herself that Hector had been the one to help her get back on her feet when she'd been just nineteen and devastated from the knife attack. He'd been the one to offer her a job and train her. She would probably be in a psych ward somewhere if it weren't for him.

She put the coffee and doughnut bag on Gabriel's desk and went out in the hall and toward Reception. Gabriel was right behind her, of course. And Hector was exactly where Cameron had said he would be. Her boss was dressed in his usual black cargo pants and black T-shirt. He'd once been special ops in the Marines, and he still looked as if he were in uniform.

Hector immediately went to her, ignoring Gabriel's scowl. Heck, Cameron was scowling now, too. Apparently, neither approved of Hector's shades-of-gray approach to his business and justice.

Hector didn't touch her. He hadn't in years, since she usually went board stiff when someone put their hands on her. But he did get close enough to whisper, "Are you all right?"

She managed a nod. "Neither of us were hit, and Gabriel has a suspect in custody."

Hector turned to Gabriel then and extended his hand. "I'm Hector March, owner of Sentry Security."

Gabriel didn't shake his hand. "I know who you are."

Hector gave a crisp nod. "And I know who you are, too, Sheriff. Why the hell would you let Jodi get anywhere near that house after we got those threatening emails?"

That grabbed Gabriel's attention. "*We?* You got an email, too?"

"Yes." Hector frowned as if annoyed that he would have to take the time to address this. "It came this morning. But Jodi got hers the day before yesterday, right after she told a reporter that she was remembering some more details of her attack. I'm sure she explained that to you, and that's why you shouldn't have let her go to the house."

"I didn't let Jodi do anything." Gabriel's voice was as crisp as Hector's nod had been. "When I saw her car, I stopped to see what she was doing. She trespassed onto private property and then stumbled onto a crime scene."

Suddenly, all eyes were on her. Even the emergency dispatcher at the reception desk and the other deputies were looking at her. Maybe they were waiting for some kind of logic from her that they would understand. But it wasn't something they'd be able to grasp. Because they'd never been left for dead in a shallow grave.

"I wanted to see if being at the old house would trigger any other memories of the night of my attack," she admitted. Best not to tell them she had also wanted to draw out the snake who'd knifed her.

Hector pulled back his shoulders, clearly not approving of that. "And did it? Are you actually remembering new details?"

"No." In fact, the only thing it had accomplished was nearly getting Gabriel, Jameson and her killed along with giving her a new set of nightmarish memories.

All that blood on the pantry floor.

Mercy, another dead body.

She prayed the man wasn't dead because of her, but Jodi had to accept that he could be.

"Did you give the FBI the email you got?" Gabriel asked Hector at the same moment that Hector asked him, "Is Jodi free to go? I can drive her to her apartment in San Antonio."

"I don't want to go home," she insisted. "I want to listen when Gabriel talks to the suspect."

Hector's mouth tightened. It was yet something else he didn't approve of. Tough. She was staying put.

"And yes, I gave the FBI the email," Hector answered Gabriel, but he kept his attention on her. "Apparently, it's not traceable since the person who sent it bounced it around through several foreign internet providers."

Not a surprise. Jodi hadn't figured it would be so easy to find out who was doing this. But then maybe their suspect would spill it all. Not just about the emails but about the person who'd hired him.

"You think the guy in custody is the one who attacked you ten years ago?" Hector asked.

She didn't jump to answer. Because she wasn't sure how much Gabriel wanted to reveal about this investigation.

"No," Gabriel finally said. "He's too young. Plus, I believe the man who attacked her has already been caught and is in prison."

Hector made a quick sound of agreement. He always did when it came to her father. It was the one thing he had in common with the Becketts—they thought her father was guilty.

"Several other people got threats," Hector went on. "Apparently, all of you did." He glanced at Gabriel, Jameson and then her. "But so did Russell Laney and August Canton."

Judging from the soft grunt of agreement Gabriel made, he was already aware of those last two. Jodi certainly wasn't, and she looked at Gabriel for him to provide some details.

"There are probably others who got the emails, too," Gabriel said as Cameron stepped away to take a call. "The FBI figures some folks just deleted them as a hoax. But, yes, I suspect anyone connected to the initial investigation was on the receiving end of the threats. Russell and August got theirs the same day I did."

Jodi knew both Russell and August, of course. Both had been suspects in the Beckett murders and her attack.

Them, and Jodi's own brother, Theo.

It was public knowledge that the police and then the FBI had questioned all three. Theo, because he'd been a hothead at the time and had a run-in that day with Gabriel's father, Sherman, over some horses that'd broken fence. Russell had gotten caught up in it simply because Jodi had ended her short relationship with him the week before the attack. August was her dad's half brother and had been just as much of a hothead as Theo.

And the cops excluded them all as suspects.

After they'd found her father passed out drunk with Gabriel's father's blood on him.

"August thinks the threatening emails prove that Travis is innocent," Hector went on. "In fact, he's already taking all of this to Travis's lawyers in the hopes that it'll help with his last-ditch appeal."

August was probably the only other person in Texas who believed her father was innocent. Despite that, it never had felt as if August and she were on the same side. That's because August had never approved of her friendship with the Becketts. It didn't matter that the friendship had ended the night of the attack. It was a drop in the bucket, though, to what August held against Jameson. Because Jameson had been the most vocal of the Becketts in professing her father's guilt.

"Theo might have gotten a threatening email, too. Have you been in touch with him?" Hector asked her.

"No. I haven't spoken to him in over a year. I don't even have a phone number for him."

Nor did she know who to contact to get one. As a DEA agent, Theo spent a lot of time on deep-cover assignments, and if the copycat/killer had managed to send Theo an email, then he or she was well connected with insider Justice Department information.

Not exactly a comforting thought if it was true.

"We have an ID on our young suspect," Cameron announced as soon as he finished his latest call. "We got a match on his prints because he's a missing person. His name is Billy Coleman."

Jodi repeated that a couple of times to see if she recognized it. She didn't.

"He's a runaway," Cameron continued. "His parents filed a missing person report about a year ago. Not for the first time, either. He's run away at least two other times. He's seventeen, and judging from his juvie record, he's paranoid schizophrenic. My guess is he's probably off his meds."

Gabriel cursed. And Jodi knew why. Billy was no doubt going to plead mental incompetence, and they might never get answers as to why he'd committed this horrible crime.

But something about that didn't sound right.

"Billy called a lawyer," Jodi pointed out.

"Yeah," Gabriel agreed, and he cursed again. "And he had the name and phone number of the attorney when he got here to the sheriff's office. Not something a runaway teen would necessarily have."

"Especially since he's not from a wealthy family," Cameron supplied. "His parents both work at blue-collar jobs."

So, that confirmed that someone had likely put Billy up to doing this, and if so, that meant he was just another victim of this tangled mess.

"What about the dead guy?" Gabriel asked Cameron. "Any ID on him yet?"

"No. His prints weren't in the system, so we'll have to try to get an ID by searching through missing person reports and getting his picture out to the press."

That might take a while. Especially if the man was homeless and no one was looking for him.

"I really think you should let me take you home," Hector said, turning back to her. "Gabriel can fill you in on anything that happens, including whatever the suspect says in the interview."

She was shaking her head before Hector even finished. "I'm staying here." And she didn't leave any room for argument in her tone.

Hector gave a heavy sigh and looked at Gabriel as if he expected him to force her to leave. "I'm not sure it's a good idea for Jodi to be out anywhere right now," Gabriel answered. "She'll be safer here."

Jodi was more than a little surprised that Gabriel had backed her up. Then she realized why he'd done that. Because she was almost certainly in danger from the person who was manipulating Billy. Gabriel probably didn't want to be a part of another attack that could leave her dead.

"Just go," Jodi told Hector. "I'll be fine."

He obviously knew that "fine" part was a lie. Was also obviously not happy about being dismissed. But he didn't get a chance to voice that unhappiness. That's because Jameson finished his phone call, and he got up from his desk, making a beeline toward them.

"There were prints on the knife," Jameson said,

"and the CSIs got an immediate hit." He snapped toward Jodi, and that definitely wasn't a friendly expression he was sporting. "Is there something you want to tell us?" he demanded.

Jodi shook her head, not understanding why Gabriel's brother looked ready to blast her to smithereens.

But she soon found out.

Jameson turned to his brother to finish delivering the news. "It's Jodi's prints on the knife."

Chapter Four

Gabriel had hoped there wouldn't be any more surprises today, but this was a huge one. Since Billy had been wearing gloves, Gabriel hadn't expected there to be any prints at all on the knife.

Especially not Jodi's.

Judging from the stunned look on her face, Jodi hadn't expected it, either. Her attention slashed from Jameson to Gabriel, and she shook her head. She also opened her mouth as if ready to blurt out some kind of denial, but the denial and anything else she might have said died on her lips because she groaned and sank down into the nearest chair.

"Jodi was obviously set up," Hector jumped to say.

Gabriel hated to give the man even a slight benefit of doubt, but Hector could be right. Of course, there was another possibility. One that wasn't going to help ease that stark expression on Jodi's already too pale face.

Gabriel moved closer to her, lifting her chin so

they could make eye contact. Like the other time he'd touched her, she tensed, making him wonder just how many "scars" she had from the attack a decade ago. Probably plenty that she wouldn't want to discuss with him.

"Do you remember ever touching the knife?" Gabriel asked. He'd chosen his words carefully. No need to say aloud that he wanted to know if she'd taken hold of the handle when her attacker had been trying to end her life.

Jodi ran her hand through her hair and shook her head. "I honestly don't know." She shifted her attention to Jameson, and even though the paleness and nerves were still there, she straightened her posture and took a deep breath. "Is the fingerprint pattern consistent with me having grabbed it while I was being stabbed?"

Jameson lifted his shoulder. "There are two clear prints. Your right index finger and thumb. The other prints are smeared."

"That means nothing. Her attacker could have been wearing gloves." Hector again.

It riled Gabriel that Jodi's boss had taken on the role of defending her. Then again, plenty of things riled him about Hector. Including the fact that Jodi had turned to him and not Gabriel after the nightmare ten years ago. Hector considered himself some kind of victim's recovery advocate and had come to visit Jodi in the hospital shortly after the attack. She'd allowed him into her life—while excluding Gabriel.

"Does Jodi need a lawyer?" Hector asked, glancing at both Jameson and Gabriel. "Are you accusing her of something? Because it certainly seems to me that's what you're doing."

Well, it hadn't been certain to Jodi. Her eyes widened, and she shook her head again.

"I know you didn't stab yourself," Gabriel said before she could speak. But that was only the tip of the iceberg. There was another component to this situation.

The most recent murder.

Jodi seemed to understand that even before Gabriel could bring it up. "I also didn't kill that man and plant the knife on the doorstep so I could clear my father's name." Jodi's voice was stronger now, and she got to her feet to face him. She repeated the part about not killing the man.

Gabriel believed her. Yeah, it was stupid to take her word at face value, especially since he'd hardly seen her in years. He wasn't sure of the woman she'd become. But he seriously doubted that Jodi had become a killer.

"The FBI wants to talk to you," Jameson told her. "They're sending an agent from their San Antonio office."

Which meant the agent would be there soon, since San Antonio was less than an hour's drive away. That might not be enough time, though, for Gabriel to get answers from their suspect. He hoped that didn't mean the agent would take her into custody.

"If this is a copycat killing," Gabriel volunteered, "then the FBI doesn't have jurisdiction. I do." That was splitting legal hairs, but it might stop Jodi from being whisked away and put through what would no doubt be grueling interrogations.

Hell.

Gabriel frowned, then silently cursed himself. He wasn't thinking with his head now. He was thinking like the twenty-four-year-old deputy who had turned Jodi away that night.

He was also thinking like a man.

One who was still attracted to a woman who shouldn't be on his attraction radar. But she was. And there didn't seem to be anything he could do about it.

"I'll get you a lawyer," Hector told her, already taking out his phone.

"No, don't. Not yet anyway." She turned back to Gabriel. "Any idea when Billy's attorney will be here?"

Gabriel had to shake his head. "But it should be soon. We've already bagged his clothes and tested his hands for gunshot residue. There's residue, by the way, and coupled with the fact that he attacked us, that'll be enough to charge him. Well, at least it's enough to charge him for shooting at us."

Jodi continued to stare at him. "You doubt that he killed that man in the house?"

Gabriel really didn't want to get into the specifics of what he thought or didn't think. Not with Hector right there. Not before he'd had a chance to try to work it all out in his head.

But there was a problem.

And Gabriel didn't believe it was his imagination that Jodi wanted to keep Hector out of this, too. Partially out of it anyway, since she'd refused to go with him and had even asked her boss to leave.

"Come with me a minute," Gabriel told her. He motioned for Jodi to follow him and headed toward the hall. He wanted her in the observation room next to where they were holding Billy.

However, Jodi didn't get far because Hector stepped in front of her, blocking her path. "You're not questioning her," Hector snapped, his glare on Gabriel.

The man knew how to test every rileable bone in Gabriel's body. "I can and I will." He tapped his badge in case Hector had forgotten that he was the one in charge here. Of course, Gabriel didn't have an interrogation in mind, but he didn't intend to tell Hector that.

"I'll be all right," Jodi told the man, and she stepped around him.

That put some fire in Hector's eyes. "It's not a good idea for you to talk to the sheriff without your lawyer present. He's abusing your childhood friendship. Hell, you might not even be able to trust him. Remember, he's the one who helped convict your father."

That stopped Jodi, and for several moments Gabriel thought she might change her mind about going with him. She took in more of those deep breaths. The kind a person took while trying to fight off a panic attack. Or a fit of temper.

"Go home," Jodi finally said to Hector. Her voice was as tight as the muscles in her face. "I'll call you when I'm done."

Oh, that didn't please Hector. That fire in his eyes turned to a full blaze. "I'm not going anywhere. I'll be waiting right here when you're finished."

In addition to being a pain, the guy was also muleheaded. Normally, Gabriel would have been pleased that Jodi had someone like that on her side, but this wasn't a normal situation. And Hector wasn't just an ordinary boss. He was someone who cut legal corners to suit his needs.

"Sorry about that," Jodi mumbled as Gabriel ushered her into the observation room.

There was a two-way mirror, and Gabriel immediately spotted Billy seated at the table in the interview room. He appeared to be asleep, his head resting on his folded arms.

Gabriel shut the door just in case Hector decided to follow them. Of course, Jameson and Cameron likely wouldn't allow that to happen. They both knew about Gabriel's low opinion of the man, and they had equally low opinions of Jodi's boss.

"Hector's protective of me," Jodi volunteered.

"Yeah, I can see that." He hadn't intended to make that sound like some kind of question, but it did. And that question was—why?

"I owe Hector," she said, answering that unspoken question. "He was there for me after, well, after."

"Only because you didn't let any of us be there for you," Gabriel pointed out.

She didn't disagree with that. Couldn't. Because she'd refused to see him, Jameson or his sisters, Ivy or Lauren, when she was home from the hospital. After that, she'd disappeared and hadn't resurfaced until eight months later at her father's trial. By then, she'd already started her association with Hector. Just how deep that association went, Gabriel didn't know.

It was possible they were or had been lovers.

Jodi didn't look away. She met his gaze head-on. "I'm stating the obvious here, but when I was recovering from my injuries, my father was charged with murdering your parents. For a while, my brother was a suspect as well, and you and Jameson were looking to put someone—*anyone*—behind bars for what happened. It didn't seem like a good idea to see you and cry on your shoulder. Plus, you had your hands full with the investigation."

"So, you cried on Hector's instead." Gabriel didn't

bother cursing himself that time, but it was definitely something he shouldn't have thrown out there. He hadn't brought her in here to dig up the past, but they were certainly doing just that.

"I cried but not on anyone's shoulder," she informed him. "Wait. You're not thinking I turned to Hector because of some romantic feelings?" She cursed, made a face and didn't wait for him to respond. "It's not like that between Hector and me. Or any other man."

Her mouth tightened as if she also had said too much. Now, she looked away, dodging his gaze, and everything in her body language signaled to him that this part of the conversation was over.

Good. It was time to move on, and he tipped his head toward Billy. "There was no blood on his clothes. Nor any visible on any part of his body."

It didn't take her long to process that. "That's why you don't believe he killed the man."

Gabriel nodded. "There was blood everywhere in that pantry, and the guy had been stabbed multiple times. An organized killer could have possibly avoided spatter, but I'm not sure Billy's anywhere near organized."

She stared at the teenager on the other side of the glass. "He could have changed his clothes and cleaned himself up after the murder." But Jodi quickly waved that off. She huffed, but it wasn't exactly a sound of frustration. There was something else mixed with it, too. "You really do know that I wouldn't do something like kill a man, don't you?"

"I know." There was something else mixed with his response, too. Empathy. Hell. More than that. Sympathy. Something that she darn sure wouldn't want him to feel. "And you do know if I'd had any suspicions ten years ago about what was going to happen, I wouldn't have let you leave my house?"

She nodded, sighed. Jodi looked up, their gazes connecting, and for just a split second, it seemed as if the last decade melted away. He caught a glimpse of the girl. The very one who'd had a thing for him. That *thing* was still there; Gabriel could feel it, but it was buried beneath the scars and the pain.

He got another flood of memories then. The heat in his own body. He'd never told Jodi that he'd wanted her that night. Wouldn't tell her, either. Because it wouldn't help. In fact, it could make things worse with them going through the "what could have been" scenarios.

Their eye contact continued, and Gabriel could feel that old attraction becoming a simmer again. Thankfully, the simmer turned chilly when he heard voices in the hall.

"I need to see the sheriff and my client now," a woman demanded. It wasn't a shout but close enough so that Gabriel had no trouble hearing her.

She was no doubt Billy's attorney. Good. That meant Gabriel could get on with the interrogation.

Gabriel threw open the door and came face-to-face with Cameron and a brunette who was dressed to the nines. She had a briefcase on the floor next to her pricey shoes. She certainly didn't look like someone who worked cheap, and that piqued his interest, and suspicions, even more. There was no way Billy could pay someone like this.

So, who was footing this bill?

"I'm Mara Rayburn," she said. Her voice had lowered a couple of notches, but she didn't sound very happy about this visit. "You're Sheriff Beckett?"

Gabriel nodded, but before he could say anything, she took his hand and slapped some papers in his palm. "That's a court order to transfer my client to a psychiatric facility where he belongs."

Heck, that was pretty fast for a court order, so Gabriel looked through it.

"It's legit," Cameron provided, sounding as suspicious about all of this as Gabriel felt. Jodi, too, because she hurried to Gabriel's side to look over the document, as well.

"How'd you get this?" Gabriel demanded. "And who's paying you?"

Mara gave him a blank stare. "I got the court order through normal channels, and as your deputy just pointed out, it's *legit.* As for who's paying me, I'm not required to divulge that information. However, you are required to comply with that court order and release my client. There's a marshal waiting outside to escort Billy to the facility, and I don't want to waste any time. Billy's a very sick young man."

"How so?" Gabriel pressed, though he already knew at least part of the answer.

Mara whipped out yet more papers from the briefcase and handed them to him. "That's a report from the psychiatrist. Billy is paranoid schizophrenic. He not only needs medication, but he also needs to be under medical supervision since he's a danger to himself."

"And others," Gabriel quickly provided.

"He fired shots at us," Jodi added. "And it's possible he killed a man."

Mara's only reaction to that was an eye roll. "Please don't tell me you're going to fight this court order. Because it won't work. Billy will get the help he needs whether you stonewall us or not."

Gabriel hitched his thumb toward Billy. "I've got a dead body, and your client is the only person who can give me answers about that."

"That's your problem, not mine, Sheriff," Mara snapped.

She motioned for someone, and a few moments later, the marshal walked up behind her. Gabriel knew him. Dallas Walker. He was a good marshal, definitely not someone who would be on the take, but he would follow through on his job. And his job would be to make sure that court order was carried out.

"Sorry about this," Dallas mumbled to Gabriel.

"No need to apologize." Mara, again. "Just get my client out of here." She turned as if to leave but then stopped and snared Gabriel's attention. "Anything my client might have said to you isn't admissible because he isn't mentally competent."

Maybe, but the jury was still out on that. "You're not doing Billy any favors by covering for the person who's manipulating him," Gabriel told the woman. "Because the person manipulating him is likely a killer. A killer who's got you on his payroll."

If she had a reaction to that, Gabriel didn't see it, because this time when she turned, she walked away. "Bring my client to the car," she added over her shoulder to the marshal.

Dallas issued another apology, and Cameron led him to the interview room. It didn't take long before the marshal was escorting him out.

Billy had a reaction all right. He smiled. "You two should be real careful," he said like a threat.

Gabriel had to rein in his temper. After all, this idiot could have killed them when they were chasing him. Plus, there was no telling what would go on in that psychiatric facility. Billy could end up not doing any time whatsoever.

"The lawyer didn't ask who I was," Jodi said under her breath.

Yeah. Gabriel had noticed that. Maybe because Mara hadn't cared enough to ask, but it could be because she already knew every single player in this. Whatever the heck *this* was.

"I'll make some calls," Cameron told them as they watched Dallas whisk Billy away. "We might be able to question him while he's at the facility."

It was a long shot, but at the moment it was all Gabriel had. Especially since they didn't even have an ID on the dead guy.

"Find out all you can about the lawyer," Gabriel told Cameron.

The deputy nodded, left to no doubt get started on that, but as Cameron was walking away, Hector was coming toward Jodi and him.

"My people just sent me a preliminary report on Mara Rayburn." Hector had his phone in his hand and appeared to be reading something on the screen. "She's thirty-two and works for a law firm in San Antonio. A reputable one."

"That doesn't mean she's reputable," Gabriel argued.

Hector made a sound of agreement and handed Gabriel his phone. Gabriel scrolled through the report, though he wouldn't take anything there at face value.

"There are no red flags," Hector concluded. "But I might be able to get financials on her."

"No." Gabriel didn't have to think about that, either. There was no legal way for them to get something like that since they didn't have probable cause on Mara. He darn sure didn't want Hector cutting corners on this and therefore compromising the entire investigation.

Jodi moved closer to Gabriel, her arm up against his as she leaned in to read the report, too. It was thorough for something classified as *preliminary*. Mara's address, phone number, educational background and even the cases she'd tried in court. As detailed as it was, Gabriel had to agree with the no red flags part. There had to be one, though, somewhere.

"Now that Billy's gone, are you ready to go home?" Hector asked her.

Gabriel looked up from the report and realized that Hector was scowling. And the man had his attention nailed to the arm-to-arm contact between Jodi and him. Jodi had said it "wasn't like that" between Hector and her, but clearly her boss had a different notion about that. Because that was pure jealousy in Hector's eyes.

Jodi noticed the jealousy, too, and the scowl. She eased away from Gabriel. "I want to stay here a little longer and see what we're able to find out."

That didn't ease Hector's expression. "You can use the resources in the office to learn anything that the sheriff can."

She lifted her shoulder, stayed put. However, Hector stayed put as well, and Gabriel thought he might have to order the man to leave. He didn't get a chance to do that, though, because he heard yet another voice.

One that he recognized this time.

Jodi did, too, and she groaned, stepping out into the hall with Gabriel right behind her. "August," she muttered like profanity.

It was indeed August Canton, her father's half brother, and he wasn't a stranger to the sheriff's office. Nope. August deemed himself as his half brother's champion of justice and was doing everything possible to get Travis out of jail. Gabriel had his own label for August—pain in the neck.

August wasn't a typical-looking uncle. For one thing, he was only a few years older than Gabriel. He was the offspring of his father's second marriage, and when his parents had been killed in a car crash when he was twelve, Travis had raised him. More or less. Travis hadn't been much of a parent to either August or Jodi, but that hadn't stopped August from standing by his brother.

And riling Jodi.

Gabriel had only heard August's side of the story on this, but according to him, Jodi wasn't doing nearly enough to clear her father's name. August apparently wanted a lot more from her. August had money, a trust fund left to him by his mother's family, and he was using a lot of his cash to pay for private investigators to dig for anything they could find. Rumor had it that it rankled him that Jodi wasn't putting in as much time and money as he was. But Jodi didn't have a trust fund. Probably didn't have the time, either, because of her job.

"What do you want?" Hector snarled at the man. Apparently, Hector knew Jodi's uncle, as well. And evidently there also wasn't any love lost between them because August's eyes narrowed to slits when he looked at Hector.

August ignored Hector's question, put his hands on his hips and studied Jodi a moment. "I heard somebody tried to kill you. You okay?"

"I'm fine." That had to be a lie, but no one challenged it. "Why are you here?" Jodi asked.

A muscle flickered in August's jaw, and he slid a glance at Hector. "I'm here because of him. Because of your boss." Definitely no friendly vibe coming from August. That tone and glance was all venom.

"Because of me?" Hector challenged.

"Yeah," August verified. "I know you're the one who nearly killed Gabriel and Jodi today."

Chapter Five

Jodi groaned. She was so used to hearing August make stupid accusations that she didn't even consider taking that one seriously.

But judging from his expression, Gabriel did.

Of course, the reason he might be doing that was because Gabriel despised her boss. However, August hadn't shown much disapproval of Hector in the past so she couldn't understand why her uncle had just accused Hector of a serious crime.

Attempted murder—of Gabriel and her, no less.

Hector stepped forward. So did Gabriel, and Jodi got in between the three of them. Not easy to do since all three were obviously primed for a fight. She was as well, but Jodi didn't think it would do any good to aim any suspicion at Hector.

"What the hell are you talking about?" Hector demanded.

Gabriel didn't say anything, but his glare should have been enough to prompt August to get talking.

"We're all in danger because of him." August tipped his head to Hector. "He's been having us watched. Followed," he added. "And he's doing that because he's afraid Jodi's remembering the truth that would blow all of this wide-open."

"What truth?" Hector spat out. Jodi wanted to know the same thing.

"The truth that will set Travis free, and if he's free, that means somebody else did those crimes. Somebody you're protecting. Don't you dare say you don't have friends or criminal informants you're trying to protect. Friends who could have killed Gabriel's folks and tried to kill Jodi."

It was so far-fetched that Jodi wanted to laugh.

"It isn't just you, me and Gabriel," August went on ranting. "Hector's had Russell tailed, too. He's on his way here now to make Hector stop."

Jodi scrubbed her hand over her face. She definitely didn't want her ex-boyfriend in on this, especially since this was all some paranoia on August's part. She turned to Hector to get him to assure August that he would never do anything like that.

Hector folded his arms over his chest and aimed a defiant stare at August. "I didn't have anything to do with the murders, and I'm not trying to protect anyone who would have done them."

What Hector didn't do was deny the other part of August's accusation, and it felt as if someone had dissolved the floor and ground beneath her feet.

No.

Hector couldn't have done that.

Gabriel cursed. "You're having us followed?" he snarled.

It took Hector several long moments to answer. "Not you. I figured you'd spot a tail right off, but I've had men on Jodi, Russell and August."

"You what?" That was all Jodi could get out because her breath suddenly got very thin.

"It was for your own safety." Hector took his hands from his hips and reached for her, but Jodi stepped back.

"Explain that," she said, and she thought her glare might match the ones August and Gabriel were giving her boss.

Hector huffed. "The person sending those threatening emails is dangerous. The murder today proves that. I figured the violence would escalate, so I wanted to keep an eye on not just you but on the most likely suspect—August."

August charged at Hector, but he didn't land the punch that he threw because Gabriel caught on to August and put him against the wall.

"Why follow Russell?" Gabriel asked Hector.

"Because he's been getting threats, too, and I thought August or someone he'd hired would go after him. You have to admit that killing Russell would be a way to shed some doubt on Travis's guilt. And

August might have an easier time killing Russell than his own niece."

"I didn't try to kill anyone," August fired back. "I just want everyone to know the truth, and that truth is my brother is innocent."

Gabriel ignored August and turned to her. "Did you know anything about Hector's spying?"

"No. Of course not. And if I had, I would have put an end to it. You had no right," she added, aiming her index finger at Hector.

She wasn't sure what riled her more—that Hector had had her followed or that she hadn't spotted the person he'd hired to do that.

"Have you forgotten that you nearly died?" Hector said. "Not just ten years ago but today, too. You're in danger, and it's not very smart to rely on the local sheriff to make sure you're safe."

Jodi stared at him. "I'm not relying on the sheriff *or you* for that. I can take care of myself. Now, call off your dogs. Not just the ones following me but the ones on August and Russell, too."

"That's not wise," Hector warned her.

"Do it!" Jodi snapped.

Hector hesitated several long moments, but he finally took out his phone to make the call. However, Gabriel stopped him.

"Did you have a tail on Jodi today?" Gabriel demanded. He didn't continue until Hector nodded. "Then ask him or her if they saw anyone go into my old family home. Anyone besides Jodi, me and a teenager wearing a ski mask."

"He didn't see anyone," Hector assured him. "I had one of my best men on Jodi. Frank," he added to her.

Frank Mendoza, former black ops. He was indeed one of Sentry's best, and it explained why she hadn't noticed him.

"Frank was positioned up the road from where Jodi parked," Hector added, "and he said he didn't see anyone go into the house except Jodi and you."

That meant the killer was there before she arrived. Watching them. Maybe committing the murder while Gabriel and she were just yards away. So much for her stellar training. She hadn't been able to sense something like that practically under her nose.

"I'll call my people now," Hector said.

"How did you find out Hector was having you followed?" Gabriel asked August the moment Hector stepped into an interview room to make his call.

"One of the PIs that I'd hired noticed it. I have security cameras everywhere—in my home, my office. Even in my car. When the PI reported to me that it appeared I was being followed, I told him to run a check on the guy and find out who he was. Imagine my surprise when I learned the tail, Rusty Millington, worked for Hector."

Of course, Jodi knew Rusty, too. He wasn't as

good as Frank, but the PI must have been top-notch to detect Rusty.

"Did you report this Rusty and Hector to the cops or the FBI?" Gabriel continued.

August frowned. "I'm reporting it now, to you, and I want you to do something about it."

"I will…if there's anything to be done. It's not a crime to follow someone, and Hector could just say he was looking out for your safety."

"Right." August didn't bother to hide the sarcasm, either. "Hector would like me out of the way so that he has Jodi completely isolated and all to himself."

Jodi was so surprised by that accusation that she flinched.

"You know it's true," August went on. "Hector's in love with you."

She shook her head. "I don't know that at all because it's not true." At least she hoped it wasn't. Hector had certainly done a lot for her, and she wanted to think it was because she did a good job for him, but she had to admit that Hector wanted more than just to be her boss. That said, she doubted he'd go to these extremes to get it.

"Am I interrupting anything?" someone asked.

Jodi had been so deep in thought that she hadn't heard the footsteps. But Gabriel clearly had because he'd already stepped in front of her. Now, he put his hand over his weapon in his side holster. But it wasn't the threat that Gabriel was gearing up for.

It was Russell.

It'd been at least six years since Jodi had seen him, but he hadn't changed much. Same blond hair and muscled body. In college, everyone had called him the golden boy because of his looks and because he excelled at sports. A city boy. The opposite of Gabriel, the cowboy cop.

But there was a different edge to Russell than there had been back in college. She knew he'd spent three years in the army, and it seemed to have hardened him a little. Put some more muscles on him, too.

"Jodi," Russell said when his attention landed on her. He went to her, his arms already reaching for her, but she motioned for him to stop.

"Uh, I don't hug," she said.

Of course, it sounded rude, but maybe Russell would get it, especially since he'd seen her in the hospital shortly after the attack. She'd had trouble with even the doctors and nurses touching her then, and in fact, Russell had been there for her first panic attack.

Plenty more had followed. And touching and hugging were triggers that she'd learned to avoid.

"Sorry," Russell said. He shook hands with August and then Gabriel. "August told you about Hector having us followed?" he asked Gabriel.

Gabriel nodded. "I also understand you got a threatening email?"

"I did, and I gave it to the FBI." Russell's forehead bunched up. "What I don't understand is why would a copycat or even Travis include me in this? Jodi and I weren't even together when your parents were killed and she was attacked."

"Lots of people are getting the threats," Jodi explained. "Who knows why? Maybe the killer thinks I told you something that could reveal his identity."

Russell glanced at Gabriel, then back at her. "So, you still think your father's innocent?"

"He is," August interrupted.

Jodi wasn't nearly as enthusiastic about that as her uncle was, but she did make a sound of agreement.

What she didn't do was offer up any details about the recent murder, about maybe it being tied to what had happened to her and Gabriel's parents. But if that knife did prove to be the murder weapon, then maybe there was some kind of DNA evidence on it to give them a suspect other than her father.

Russell kept his attention on her. "How are you? I'm guessing what happened today shook you up?"

"Some. I'm okay," Jodi lied. "How about you? I understand you got married?"

Russell flashed that golden-boy smile that had first attracted her to him, but there was no trace of that attraction now. She thought that was mutual, too. "I married a wonderful woman four years ago. I met her not long after I left the army. And I'm a dad. Our son is six months old." The smile faded. "My wife and son are the reason I'm so upset about that threatening email. I don't want anyone going after them because of what went on between us."

Jodi heard the anger just beneath the surface. Anger maybe aimed at her because if he hadn't gone on three dates with her, then none of this would be happening right now. But the anger was warranted because Russell was no doubt concerned about this monster going after his wife and child.

"San Antonio police know about the threat," Russell continued, "and August encouraged me to beef up security. I did. I had a new security system installed, and I've told my wife not to go out of the house without me." The muscles in his face got tight. "Obviously, I don't want to have to live like this much longer, so just how close are you to catching this dirtbag?" He directed that question to Gabriel.

Gabriel shrugged. "There is a suspect. Once I'm able to question him, I'll know more."

"I want to talk to him," Russell said, and it was a demand. August nodded in agreement.

Now it was Gabriel's jaw muscles that got tight. "Not a chance. Unless you two become law enforcement officers, you're not getting anywhere near him. I don't want anything to compromise this investigation. Because if that happens, this guy could be guilty as sin and still walk."

August opened his mouth, probably to argue with that, but he didn't have time to say anything before Hector came out of the interview room.

"I've called off the surveillance for all of you," Hector said, "but there's a problem." He paused. "Someone broke into Jodi's apartment."

Her breath froze, and she felt the instant slam of fear. "When?"

"I'm not sure, but he sent me this." Hector handed her his phone, and she saw the photo on the screen.

It was a selfie from the looks of it. A sick one. Because the person was wearing a ski mask identical to the one their teenage suspect had on when they'd found him. In the background, she could see her bedroom. The clothes that she'd left on the bed. The coffee cup on the dresser. She could also see something else.

The knife the man was holding up in his left hand.

It was a crescent blade with a broken tip.

She choked back a gasp just in time, and if Hector hadn't taken the phone from her, she might have dropped it. Gabriel snatched the phone from Hector, looked at it and cursed.

"When's the last time you were home?" Gabriel asked.

It took her a moment to gather her breath and her composure. Jodi felt the panic fade, replaced by the anger of having someone do this. "Early this morning. He must have gotten in after I left for work."

Russell and August looked at the picture, too. "Or maybe this creep was in your place ages ago," August pointed out.

Jodi had to shake her head. "No, those are the clothes that I put there this morning, and that's the coffee mug I used."

"The FBI is headed to your place," Hector explained. "They'll process the crime scene. And this photo."

Yes, because sometimes there were bits of hidden data in digital pictures. Maybe they'd get lucky. But she doubted this intruder had been sloppy enough to leave a trace of himself behind.

Gabriel glanced at Hector, then Jodi. "How the hell did he get past your security system?"

Good question. Because she had a good system. The best, as a matter of fact—complete with motion detectors and cameras. And she looked at Hector to see if he had an answer for that since he'd been the one to install it.

"Any chance your hired spy gave the intruder the code so he could waltz right into Jodi's apartment?" August asked Hector.

Hector's eyes were narrowed to slits when he turned to August. "No. Any chance your PIs could have found the code and given it to him?"

Oh, no. This was about to get ugly.

"Or maybe you gave that thug the code," August added, and yes, he aimed that accusation at Hector.

"Why the hell would I do that?" Hector snapped.

"To send Jodi running to you. To make her believe that you're the one who can protect her."

That went back to August's theory of Hector trying to isolate her from everyone but him, but obviously it was a theory that ticked off Hector. Since she didn't want punches thrown, she stepped between them again. However, that didn't stop Hector. He just charged right past her, and it might have come to blows if Gabriel hadn't taken hold of Hector. Russell did the same to August.

"I'm not going to stand here and have this moron accuse me of junk like that." Hector's voice was past the anger stage now, and the veins in his neck were bulging. Jodi had never seen him like this, but then August was a pro at pressing hot buttons.

"You," Gabriel said, pointing to August. "Leave now. You two, as well," he added to Hector and Russell.

Russell gladly obliged. In fact, he looked plenty sorry that he'd even made this trip. August, however, didn't go so easily. He spat out some profanities, looking at Jodi as if he wanted her to intervene on his behalf.

She wouldn't.

"You need to go," she told him.

That didn't please August, and it earned her a few choice curse words from him, but her uncle finally stormed out. It didn't surprise her, though, when Hector stayed put.

"You can't go back to your apartment," he said.

Of course, Jodi knew that, but there'd been so

much info for her to process that it took her a couple of moments to realize the next thing Hector was about to point out—that she had to go somewhere safe.

But where?

She'd been trained to fight and shoot, but that wouldn't stop someone from gunning her down. Or worse. It wouldn't stop a monster from killing Gabriel, Russell or someone else just to prove a point. Exactly what point, she didn't know, but anyone who'd gotten a threatening email was at risk. She couldn't protect them all. Neither could Hector or Gabriel.

"I want you to come to my house," Hector insisted. "Or to the office. I can have both guarded 24/7."

Jodi was shaking her head before he even finished. Maybe the unease she was feeling was because Hector had had her followed without telling her. Or maybe nearly being killed had created this edgier-than-usual feeling inside her. Either way, she wasn't going with him.

"Thanks, but no thanks," she answered.

If this snake had managed to get someone into her apartment, he could get to her anywhere. Including the fortress that Hector called home.

Hector's stare turned to a glare that he shifted from her to Gabriel. It was the exact reaction she expected. Some anger mixed with disappointment.

Hector wasn't stupid, and he had to have known she was picking sides. A side that would help her get to the bottom of this while not being killed.

And that *side* was with Gabriel.

Hector turned to leave but then stopped. "Gabriel didn't save you ten years ago. Just remember that," Hector said like a warning before he walked out.

Jodi waited to see if Gabriel was going to respond to that. He didn't. He just stood there, hands on his hips, watching as Hector went out of the building.

"I didn't tell Hector that I went to your house that night ten years ago," she explained. "He didn't know I'd come on to you and that you'd turned me down."

Jodi didn't want Gabriel to think she had poured her heart out to Hector. She hadn't. She hadn't poured out her heart to anyone.

Gabriel's silence continued for several more moments before he looked at her. "How exactly did you meet Hector?"

She'd expected questions, just not that one, and she didn't miss that he'd used his lawman's tone to ask it.

"He came to the hospital about a week after the stabbing." It wasn't hard to recall that meeting. In fact, those days, and the physical pain, were as fresh as if it'd just happened. "He said he'd read about the attack, and he wanted to offer me help getting back on my feet."

Gabriel made a sound of sarcastic disapproval,

probably because she hadn't accepted any assistance from him, his sisters or her friends. Including Russell, who'd told her he would be there for her in any way he could. But Hector had offered her something no one else had.

"Hector said he could train me in self-defense, that he could teach me to use a firearm. A knife," Jodi softly added. "Everyone but the FBI was skirting around my attack, but Hector talked about it head-on. He said once I was trained that I could work for him, and that no one would be able to hurt me like that again."

There it was in a nutshell. Jodi would have trusted almost anyone who'd made her believe that she could not only recover but that she would also never again be a victim.

She wouldn't be, either.

The next person who tried to put their hands on her was going to pay.

"And you didn't believe it was suspicious that a stranger would show up and make an offer like that?" Again, he sounded like a lawman, one who had his own doubts.

"What are you asking?"

"If you think Hector could have orchestrated this," Gabriel answered without hesitation.

"No. He didn't know me before the original attack—"

"You're positive?" he snapped.

Well, she had been until now. After giving it some thought, she had to shake her head again. "Hector's not connected to your parents…is he?"

"Not that I know of, but you can bet I'll be checking to see." He looked at her again. "Someone must have given the intruder the code to get past your security system. I'm not saying Hector did that," he quickly added, "but it could have been one of his employees. Someone who's close to both Hector and you."

A person who might have tried to kill them today.

And that someone might have murdered his parents.

"I know you've gone over every case file your father had worked on," she reminded him. "Were you able to exclude everyone connected to his investigations?"

"No." He cursed and rubbed the back of his neck. "There was a file with notes about Hattie Osmond that didn't make sense."

"Hattie?" she asked. Jodi knew the woman. Or rather, had known her. Hattie was a widow and had owned a big ranch not far from Gabriel's. She'd stayed pretty much to herself until she'd passed away a couple of years ago.

"My dad thought Hattie was being swindled or else blackmailed," Gabriel explained. "She was selling off her livestock and was making weekly trips to the bank."

Yes, that would have been out of the ordinary for her. "Maybe she was sick or wanted to spend her money on her family."

"That's just it. She didn't have a family. I'm talking no heirs except for some distant cousins who didn't even know her. Anyway, when she died, her estate was valued at a fraction of what everyone thought she had, and she'd destroyed a lot of records that people normally keep."

Jodi tried to figure out where he was going with this. "You think Hector was involved in that?"

"Maybe. But your father could have been, too. Or August. Hell. Anybody could have been. It might not even be connected to anything. It's just a loose end, and right now loose ends are all I've got to figure this out."

"Yes," she softly agreed. "And it might be hours or days before you can get in to see Billy Coleman."

Hours that she could be using to find out who'd gotten into her apartment and if Hector did indeed have any old ties that she should know about. While she was at it, she could maybe sneak in to see Billy.

"Do you still have a break room here in the sheriff's office?" she asked. "Because my nerves are a little shot, and I could use some rest."

Gabriel stared at her as if trying to figure out if that was the truth. It wasn't.

"I need my meds," she added, since it was obvious he wasn't going to buy anything other than the truth. Jodi went with a half lie. "I came really close to a panic attack earlier, and the meds are the only thing that'll help. Unfortunately, they sometimes make me drowsy."

More staring, then he nodded and tipped his head to the left side of the building. "The break room is still there. I'll let you know if I hear anything about Billy or the knife."

The knife. She certainly hadn't forgotten about that. Especially since her prints were on it. But that was yet another reason for her to get the heck out of there. The FBI might try to take her into custody while they got that all sorted out. No way did she want to spend hours waiting in an interview room.

Jodi made her way through the building, one that she knew like the back of her hand. That's because she'd come here often enough with Ivy. First, just because Ivy's dad would give them money for ice cream. Then, later, Jodi came so she could flirt with Gabriel.

Not that he'd flirted back.

But she hadn't given up. Not until that night ten years ago anyway.

The break room was just as it had been the last time she was there. Same old leather sofa. Same fridge from the looks of it. Judging from the smells in the air, someone had recently eaten pizza and had coffee.

There were two ways out—the emergency exit

and a window. The door had an alarm on it. It was nothing fancy—just something to alert the lawmen if it opened. Since Jodi didn't want to do that, she checked out the window. No obvious wires or sensors to indicate it was connected to the security system, so she unlocked it and lifted it a fraction.

No alarm.

If it had gone off, she could have told Gabriel she just needed some fresh air. At least now she wouldn't need to lie to his face.

Jodi lifted the window the rest of the way up, pushed out the screen and shimmied outside. She started running the moment her feet landed on the ground.

She didn't get far. The moment she rounded the corner, she smacked right into someone.

Gabriel.

"Back inside," he snarled. Before she had a chance to protest, he took hold of her arm, his grip hard. "You're under arrest."

Chapter Six

This was the first time that Gabriel had brought someone in his custody to his family's ranch. Of course, it was also possibly the first time he'd arrested someone because he was pissed off at them.

It'd been stupid—along with being dangerous—for Jodi to try to run from him, but he'd known from the moment she said she needed a nap that she was going to try to sneak out of the sheriff's office. And if he'd let her out of his sight, she would have tried it again. That's why he'd arrested her, so he could hold her as a witness in his criminal investigation.

Even though Gabriel wouldn't want to have to explain himself to a judge, he was on solid legal ground. As the sheriff, he had a right to compel someone to give a statement if they'd witnessed a crime. He could do that by detaining them, and while detention and protective custody might keep Jodi alive, it wasn't winning him any brownie points with her.

Not that he wanted points, that is.

Gabriel would settle for her just not glaring at him. And for her being safe. God, he needed for her to be safe.

If he'd trusted Hector, that might be the best place for her, but there were too many questions about the man. Taking Jodi there could be walking her right into the lion's den. Although Gabriel wasn't doing much better by her. He was taking her back to the scene of the crime.

Less than a quarter of a mile from it anyway.

"I shouldn't be here," she said the moment he pulled to a stop in front of his house. It didn't help that it was late, and the muggy heat was practically smothering them. Conditions that were almost identical to that night when she'd been left for dead.

From his truck window, she looked up at the bright moon. Yet another thing that had been in place during the attack. Too bad it hadn't given her enough light to have seen her attacker's face. If she had, then she might be convinced that her father was a killer. Of course, that wouldn't help them with a copycat, but now that Billy was locked up, at least they didn't have to worry about him.

He hoped.

"It's just for tonight," Gabriel assured her. "I can make other arrangements for you tomorrow." Along with having one of the deputies get her car. Right now, it was still parked on the road near the old house. He definitely didn't want to go there tonight.

"*I* can make other arrangements," she insisted.

"Yeah, I'm sure you can, but I didn't think you'd want to be alone."

Jodi didn't argue with that, though that's likely what she wanted to do. After all, she could have reminded him that she lived alone and had for the past decade. But this wasn't an ordinary night.

"I know you don't want anyone to realize that you seeing the knife and the dead body shook you to the core," he went on. "That's probably because you think I'll take it as a sign of weakness. I wouldn't," he assured her.

"Yet you felt I was weak enough to bring me here," she huffed, pushing her hair from her face. "And I was weak enough to let you do it."

Now, Gabriel huffed. Definitely no brownie points. "Come on in. You can grab a shower, rest or eat. Whatever you want. I'll call and see if there's an update on the knife."

Some of the anger eased in her eyes when she looked at him. "Thank you."

Well, it was a start, and Gabriel took that as a green flag to get her moving out of the truck and onto the porch. Every step had to be a trip down memory lane for her. That's why he hurried and got her inside. There shouldn't be any of those memories of that night in the house since they'd had their short conversation on the porch.

The conversation where he'd turned her down.

He looked at her just as she looked at him, and he saw that she was reliving that little chat, too. And judging from the way her eyebrow lifted, she was maybe waiting for him to say something about it. But what he could say? Nothing that would make this better, that's for sure.

"I thought I was doing the right thing that night," he finally admitted. "I thought I was doing you a favor."

She laughed. Not from humor. Because there wasn't anything funny about what he was saying. Ironic that doing what he thought was the right thing had nearly gotten her killed.

Gabriel wouldn't be able to forget that. Ever.

Jodi went past him and into the living room. She glanced around, maybe noticing that he'd had the place redecorated. It was more him now and not just the house he'd inherited from his grandparents.

"Is the downstairs guest room still where it used to be?" she asked.

He nodded, and she immediately headed up the hall toward it. Only then did Gabriel release the breath he'd been holding. She was staying, for now, but just in case she decided to climb out the window, he set the security system. All the windows and doors were wired to sound the alarm if someone opened any of them. However, the only sound he heard was when she turned on the shower.

Gabriel went into the kitchen, put some sandwiches together and got started on checking for updates.

Nothing.

Well, nothing good anyway. Billy had been checked into the facility and wouldn't be evaluated by the psychiatrist until tomorrow morning. Heaven knew how long it would be before Gabriel could see him after that. Maybe not at all if the shrink deemed him incompetent.

That left Billy's lawyer and the knife.

There was no proof yet as to who was paying the attorney, and the knife was just as much of a puzzle as it had been when Gabriel had seen it on the doorstep of the old house. Jodi's prints combined with the dead guy's blood. Definitely not a good combination.

The broken tip appeared to be a match for the weapon used to kill both his parents and the man they found, but the lab would have to test both to be certain. Maybe during that testing, the techs could confirm whether Jodi's prints had been left there that night or if they'd been planted on it later. And he was certain if it was the latter that someone had indeed planted them. Because Jodi wasn't a killer.

Gabriel had just taken a bite of his sandwich when he heard a strange sound. A gasp, maybe. Definitely not something he wanted to hear. He ran to the guest room, praying that nothing was wrong. He knocked and tested the knob to find it locked. He was just on edge enough to break it down, but that wasn't necessary because Jodi opened it.

The lights were off in the bedroom, the shower still running in the adjoining bathroom, but Jodi was there. She hadn't run away after all, though she certainly looked ready to bolt.

Along with only being partly dressed.

Her jeans were on the bed, no doubt where she'd tossed them before taking her shower. Even though her top was long enough to cover her panties, Gabriel still noticed plenty of her bare legs. Jodi didn't seem to notice since her attention was on the other side of the room. Judging from her stark expression, something had spooked her.

"I thought I saw someone." She had a firm grip on her gun, but she took him by the hand and practically dragged him to the window. Not that she had to work hard to do that. Gabriel headed there while drawing his own weapon.

She didn't go directly in front of the window but instead stood to the side and peered out. Gabriel did the same.

And he cursed.

He rarely went in this room and hadn't realized it had a view of the old house. The moonlight was glinting off the tin roof of the place. It was like a beacon in the night and looked more than a little creepy.

"It might have just been a shadow," she said, her

voice a breathy whisper. A whisper that was filled with nerves.

Gabriel tried to pick through the darkness and see if he could spot anyone. There used to be plenty of shrubs that lined the path between his place and the house. He'd had a lot of them cut down after that night because Jodi's attacker had used them to sneak up on her. He hadn't liked the idea of keeping something like that around. But over the years, some cedars had popped up. They were full and bushy, making them a perfect place for someone to hide.

"I don't suppose Ivy, Lauren or Jameson would be out there at this time of night?" Jodi asked.

"No. Jameson built a big log cabin by the river." It was a good half mile from here, and besides, he was still at work. "Ivy left the week after our parents were killed and hasn't been back to the ranch. Lauren didn't come back after she went off to college." He paused. "I figured you knew about Ivy since you two were so close."

Jodi's shoulders stiffened. "No. I haven't seen or heard from her."

Too bad. "Other than the occasional Christmas card and email, she hasn't stayed in touch with anyone. She left around the time that she and your brother broke up."

"Yes," she said under her breath. "They were in love. Or at least they thought they were. Theo blamed

Ivy for not believing he was innocent of the murders. He thought she'd put you up to bringing him in for questioning."

Ivy hadn't, but then she hadn't exactly jumped to defend Theo, either. Gabriel wasn't sure why, but in the end Theo's name had been cleared, and he'd gone on to be a DEA agent. All had worked out as well as it could for those two. But Gabriel knew his sister was still broken in some ways. Maybe clinging to the past, too, since Ivy had been the one to insist they not tear down the old house. Of course, she'd insisted that years ago, so maybe it was time to revisit that issue. He didn't like having the nightmare staring him right in the face every day when he drove past it.

His folks would hate that he hadn't been able to keep the family together. Would hate even more that Gabriel hadn't tried too hard to bring his sisters back home. But in the moments when it ate away at him, he rationalized that they had their own lives. Maybe not especially good ones since both Ivy and Lauren had lost their partners.

Yeah, his dad and mom wouldn't care for him not stepping up to the parent role. But Gabriel hadn't seen any reason to drag them back to a place where the memories might be more than his kid sisters could handle. Hell. Sometimes, it was too much for him to handle.

Gabriel continued to look around, also glancing at Jodi to make sure she wasn't about to go into panic attack mode. She wasn't. But her attention kept going back to that section of the trail where she'd nearly died.

"I remember so many things about that night," Jodi said, breaking the silence. "Except for his face."

He remembered plenty of things, too, even though there were times when he wished he didn't. Gabriel certainly remembered finding Jodi. Later he'd had to piece together what had happened to her when she'd left his house that night.

After her attacker had cut her up, he'd dragged her just off the trail and put her in a makeshift "grave" that he'd dug out with his own hands. It really was just a couple of inches of topsoil that the person had scraped away, and then he'd tried to cover her body with some dirt and leaves.

It'd been a miracle that Gabriel had even seen her, especially since by then he'd gotten the frantic call from Ivy to let him know that something "bad" had gone on at the house. After hearing Ivy say that, his focus had been on getting to the house.

Fast.

Gabriel had started running immediately after Ivy's call, and if he hadn't looked down at the exact moment he did, he might not have seen the blood on the ground. He might not have even looked at the grave where the killer had put Jodi.

She could have died right there in that spot.

"I guess it was a false alarm," she added several moments later. "I don't see anyone out there."

Neither did he, but he didn't budge. Jodi did, though. She went into the bathroom to finish getting dressed, but as soon as she'd done that, she hurried straight back to the window.

"Did you get any new info on the investigation?" she asked.

"Not yet. Maybe by morning we'll have something, though." He paused. "You should know that I'll be investigating Hector, to see if he had any connection to our dead guy. Any connection to Hattie, as well."

Jodi didn't seem to have any objections to that. Maybe because she was still upset at her boss having her followed. "August knew her, too, of course."

True. Hattie had lived just up the road from Jodi's family. Gabriel had looked for anything obvious to link August, and anyone else, to Hattie. Now, he needed to dig even deeper because, so far, he hadn't found anything.

"You think August could have killed your father because he was investigating him," she said. It wasn't a question, but if it had been, the answer would have been—it was possible.

"At the time of the murders, August was twenty-eight, broke," Gabriel explained. "He didn't get his trust fund until he was thirty, two years later. He could have milked money from Hattie to pay for all those things he couldn't afford. August always had expensive tastes in cars, women and clothes."

All of that was purely circumstantial, though, and it didn't mean Travis was innocent. Travis could have still murdered Gabriel's parents, and August could have been an accessory.

It could have even been August who'd attacked Jodi.

She tipped her head to the bathroom, probably to say that it was time to put an end to this impromptu surveillance and finish getting cleaned up, but she didn't speak. Something had caught her eye. Just as it'd caught Gabriel's.

There was some movement on the road in front of the old house.

Not a shadow. It was either a deer or a person. The knot in Gabriel's stomach told him it wasn't a deer.

"Wait here," he told her. "I'll get some binoculars."

He didn't remind her to stay back from the glass because Jodi was already doing that. But he did hurry. Whatever he'd seen wasn't coming their direction, but that could change. He didn't have any night goggles and made a mental note to bring a pair to the house, but he had the standard ones that his dad had used for hunting. Gabriel brought them back to the window and had a look at the spot where he'd seen the movement.

"Nothing," he relayed to Jodi, and he handed her the binoculars so she could check it out for herself. Several moments later she made a sound of agreement. That sound was coupled with some relief, too.

Gabriel took out his phone. "I'll have one of the deputies go by the place just in case."

Even though the CSIs had already processed the pantry and kitchen, he didn't want any thrill seekers trying to get a look at the crime scene. He also didn't want to leave Jodi alone so he could do it himself.

"Wait. It's a man," Jodi said, quickly passing him back the binoculars. No relief now. There was an edge and an urgency in her voice. "He's by the cluster of trees just up the road from your parents' house. He's wearing a ski mask."

That knot in his stomach had been warranted after all, and he had a look for himself. Yeah, he saw someone all right. And the person was on the move. Not leaving, either. The guy was coming in the direction of Gabriel's place.

He handed Jodi the binoculars so he could text Cameron, and he warned the deputy to approach with caution. Since this clown had on a ski mask, this might not be a prank situation after all. It could be the person who'd put Billy up to killing a man and then attacking Jodi and him.

"He's got a gun," Jodi blurted out.

Gabriel had just finished the text, and he pushed her away from the window and against the wall. She automatically pushed back and brought up both her knee and hand as if to fight him. Gabriel eased away from her, hoping it would lessen the panic he suddenly felt in her. The panic hadn't come from the guy with the gun, though. It had come because he'd touched her.

Now, Gabriel had a whole new reason to hate her father. Or whoever the hell it was who'd gone after her with that knife. The attack had left her this way, and after all these years, it might be permanent.

"I just didn't want you in this guy's line of sight," he reminded her.

She nodded and lowered both her knee and her hand. At least she hadn't tried to shoot him. With her training and skills, she might have managed to get off a shot before he could stop her.

Gabriel went back to the window, only glancing at Cameron's text response that he was on the way. It took him a moment to spot the guy again. He was definitely coming toward the house, and he was running now. It would be only a couple of minutes before he got there.

He weighed his options and doubted he'd be able to convince Jodi to hide in the bathroom. That meant Gabriel just had to protect her as best he could.

"Go in the living room and disarm the security system," he told her and rattled off the code. "Otherwise, when I open this window, the alarm will go off, and I won't be able to hear."

Gabriel especially needed to hear if this guy had brought a partner in crime with him. One that was even closer to the house than this one.

Jodi didn't question his order. She ran out of the room, and Gabriel didn't take his attention off the thug. The moment Jodi made it back, he threw open the window and took aim. He waited a couple more seconds, until the man was plenty close enough.

"Stop and put your hands in the air," Gabriel shouted.

Judging from the way the guy snapped back his shoulders, Gabriel had surprised him. What the idiot didn't do was put up his hands. Nor did he stop. He started running, not toward the house but to his right. There were thick woods back there, and Gabriel didn't want him getting away.

"Stay here," he told Jodi.

He didn't figure she would, and she didn't. She was right on his heels and followed him to the door. Gabriel opened it, looking out to make sure he wasn't about to be ambushed. When he didn't see anyone, he hurried to the side of the porch that would give him the best view of the trespasser.

"Stop or I'll shoot," Gabriel called out.

The guy did stop, but he didn't look up at Gabriel. Instead he glanced in the direction of the road in front of the old house. Specifically, he glanced at Jodi's car that was still parked there.

That bad feeling in Gabriel's gut went up a huge notch. His gut was right. Because Jodi's car exploded into a ball of flames.

Chapter Seven

Jodi had hoped a long shower would help loosen her tense muscles. No such luck, though. Sleep hadn't helped, either. Too many dreams. Too many nightmarish images. She had the nightmares so often that they were part of what she now considered normal, but sometimes it was next to impossible to deal with her "normal."

Being around Gabriel wasn't helping with those memories, but even with that weighing her down, Jodi had to admit there was something comforting about having him nearby. Which, of course, only put her on edge even more. She'd learned the hard way that when you let down your guard, you got hurt. That's why she needed to make arrangements for a safe place to stay.

Clearly, that wasn't the ranch.

Though Gabriel had disagreed with that. He'd talked her into staying the night mainly because of the bomber still being out there. He had beefed up security by having two reserve deputies patrol the area, and Gabriel had stayed in the guest room with her. Guarding her.

From the floor.

That's where he'd put his makeshift bed, but Jodi doubted he'd gotten much sleep. She certainly hadn't.

She dressed in the loaner clothes Gabriel had left for her in the bathroom. Jeans and a loose gray top. She hoped these were things that Ivy had left behind because she didn't like the idea of wearing something from one of his ex-girlfriends.

Or maybe he even had a current girlfriend.

Gabriel hadn't mentioned one, but it was possible that his "normal" included things like dating and relationships. A life. Something she hadn't quite managed to get since she'd been put in that shallow grave.

After she combed her hair, Jodi made her way to the kitchen, where she'd left Gabriel. He was still there but not alone. Jameson and Cameron were seated with him at the breakfast table. She didn't catch what they were saying, and they hushed when they spotted her.

"What's wrong?" she asked. Because judging from their expressions, there'd been either another murder or a serious hitch in the investigation.

Gabriel got up, poured her a cup of coffee and motioned for her to sit. Jodi took the coffee, but she stood. She'd found that pacing usually worked a lot better than being seated if she was about to have to take another mental punch.

"There's been no sign of the bomber," Gabriel said.

Not good but it was something she'd expected. Gabriel and Jameson had searched for several hours after leaving Cameron at the house to watch her. They'd found nothing and called it a night. Now that the sun had been up for several hours, she'd hoped they would find some evidence that would lead them to him. Apparently not.

"There was a security camera in your car," Gabriel added.

With everything going on, she'd forgotten about that. "It's motion activated, and the feed goes to a storage cloud. Please tell me you saw the guy on there."

Gabriel shook his head. "The bomber managed to jam the feed."

She took a long sip of coffee, her grip too tight on the cup, but at least it stopped her from gasping, trembling or doing something else to make them think she was losing it. But this was critical. Jamming a camera like that would take some expertise and the right equipment. It meant this hadn't been done by some amateur thrill seeker.

"Billy's still locked up and didn't have any computer or phone access," Jameson explained. "That means he's probably not the one who sent this thug."

"His lawyer could have," she quickly pointed out. "Or the person who hired the lawyer for him."

Jameson nodded. "We're looking into it." He didn't sound very hopeful they'd come up with that, but at least it was a lead. Maybe the only one they had right now.

"Why would anyone blow up my car?" she threw out there. "It was obvious I wasn't in it, hadn't been in it for hours. So, if he wasn't trying to kill me, what was the point?"

"To scare you," Gabriel readily answered. "To send you into a panic so that you did something dangerous like run outside so you could be shot."

Jodi heard the disapproval in Gabriel's voice. Disapproval since she had indeed gone outside, but she hadn't panicked. Now, she sat down in the chair next to him and tried to piece her thoughts together.

"If this is a copycat, he'll want to re-create what happened that night," she suggested. "Not just by coming after me but also by killing someone else in the house."

No one at the table disagreed with that. It wasn't exactly a settling thought to have three lawmen admit that someone could want to slice her up again. But there was something in Gabriel's eyes that told her there was more to this than a simple copycat crime.

"We got some of the lab results on the knife," Gabriel continued a moment later. "It's the same one used to murder my parents and attack you. The broken tip was a perfect match to it."

That caused the skin to crawl on the back of her neck. Since she was fighting to tamp down the flashbacks, Jodi was sorry she'd sat down, but she couldn't stand back up. Her legs suddenly felt wobbly.

"And the blood and prints on the knife?" she asked.

"The blood belongs to the guy we found in the pantry." Gabriel looked at her again. "The only prints on it are yours. The lab said they look like defensive prints."

In other words, she had managed to grab the knife that night. That meant she must have seen her attacker's face. Of course, she'd known all along that was possible, but hearing it spelled out made her want to remember even more. If she could just see his face, then it could prove her father hadn't been the one to try to kill her.

Maybe.

And it just might confirm his guilt. But at least she would know. *Her father* would know, since he'd been too drunk to recall much of what'd gone on that night.

"The obvious question is—where has the knife been this whole time?" Jameson asked. "It didn't show any signs of being out in the elements. Or buried."

Jameson glanced at her, maybe to make sure those

two words hadn't been too much for her to handle. After all, she'd been buried. But Jodi was pushing away the memories and the panic so she could concentrate on what this new information might mean.

"The killer—or his accomplice," she quickly amended, "could have had it hidden all this time. Then, when I leaked it to the press that I was remembering details of the attack, maybe he freaked out and decided to try to scare me off."

"Or someone could have found the knife shortly after the attacks, kept it and decided to use it to play a sick game with you," Gabriel commented.

Yes, and that led her right back to August. Even if he hadn't been an accomplice or the killer, August might have found the knife near the scene and kept it, believing that it would incriminate her father. Ironic that it only had her prints and not the person responsible for this nightmarish crime.

Cameron finished his cup of coffee and stood. "I'll head to the sheriff's office and see if I can come up with anything on Billy's lawyer."

Jameson stood as well, and looked at Gabriel. "And I'll drive into San Antonio and find out who I can press to get one of us an interview with Billy."

Gabriel thanked them both. Cameron left, but Jameson lingered behind and aimed some glances at both Jodi and him. "You're both welcome to stay at my place. That way, you won't have to be so close to the old house. I suspect the CSIs will be all over it and the grounds."

They would be, but she had to shake her head. "Thanks for the offer, but I have some places in mind where I can go."

Jodi didn't, not yet anyway, but she would. She'd kept money in her apartment and car, but since she couldn't get to either of those, she would need to go to a bank. Once she had some cash, she could check into a hotel under a fake name and then figure out what her next step was. She didn't want to be tucked away where she couldn't investigate this, but she couldn't allow herself to be an easy target, either.

Jameson made a "suit yourself" sound and walked out. Gabriel got up, too, and followed him. So he could set the security system, Jodi realized. She hadn't needed a reminder of the danger, but that did it. So did Gabriel's expression. It was somehow wired and weary at the same time, and he coupled it with a huff.

"What places?" Gabriel asked, coming back into the kitchen. He went straight to the coffeepot and poured himself another cup.

It took her a moment to realize he was asking her where she had in mind to go. "A friend's house," she lied. "Not Hector's," she quickly added. That wasn't a lie. She had no intention of going there.

Gabriel huffed again, and it was louder than his earlier one. "You have nightmares," he said. "I heard you talking in your sleep, so don't deny it. You've admitted you have panic attacks. Someone tried to kill you, then broke into your apartment and blew up your car. I'm thinking *a friend's house* isn't the place you should be going."

He was right, of course. Even if she had any close friends, she couldn't bring the danger to their doorstep. Besides, judging from Gabriel's tone, he was thinking *friend* meant *lover*.

"You can't believe it's a good idea for me to stay here." But as soon as she said it, Jodi realized something. Maybe it was a good idea.

If she wanted a final confrontation with this monster.

And she did.

Everything happening seemed to be leading back to this place. To the scene of the original crime. Maybe her attacker wanted to finish what he'd started here. Well, she wanted to finish it, too, but with a totally different ending than this sick piece of slime had planned. This time, she wanted to be the one to end his life and put a stop to the danger once and for all.

"Fine," she amended. "I'll stay here."

Gabriel lifted his eyebrow, stared at her. Obviously, he knew what she was doing. But there was no way he could turn her down. Not this time. In fact, after what'd happened ten years ago, he might never turn her down again. Maybe Jodi could use that to bring all of this to a close.

He got in her face. So close that she had no trouble seeing all those flecks of silver in his blue eyes. "You might think you're ready to face down a killer, but it can't go past the thinking stage. Got that?" His jaw was tight. His words spoken through clenched teeth. "I don't want you outside on your own. And I don't want you on the trail that leads between here and my parents' house. I especially don't want you doing anything stupid like making yourself bait."

She shook her head and didn't dodge his intense stare. "You have to admit I'm the ultimate bait. I'm the one he wants."

Gabriel cursed. "You don't know that. Whoever killed that man could be trying to free your father by going after me or my brother. Especially if it's August."

True, and Jodi hated that she didn't know the reason behind all of this. Hated even more that her own kin could be responsible.

And that wasn't all that was causing her nerves to go into overdrive.

There was one more facet to this, especially if she did indeed stay here for another night or two. The attraction. She looked at Gabriel to see if that had occurred to him.

It had.

"It's easy for me to lose focus around you," Gabriel readily admitted, surprising her. Maybe surprising himself, too. "That can't happen. Because it could get one of us killed."

Jodi nodded. With that clarified, she should have looked away, probably should have just excused herself and gone back to the guest room to start making some calls to help with the investigation. But she stayed put.

Gabriel did, as well.

And, mercy, the heat came. She could feel it swirling between them. They'd never kissed, something she regretted simply because it made her want to do that now. Jodi wanted to know the feel of his mouth on hers. His taste. She was betting Gabriel was a good kisser, and there was the problem. With the heat and spent adrenaline already in play, it wouldn't stop with just a single kiss.

No, they'd land in bed.

At least, her body would want them to end up there, but Jodi was betting her mind wouldn't let things get that far. Heck, it was possible the kiss would even trigger a panic attack.

That reminder caused her to step back, though it wasn't necessary. Gabriel's phone rang, the sound slicing through the room—and the heat from the attraction—and he moved back as well to answer it. He didn't put the call on speaker, so she couldn't hear what the caller was saying, but whatever it was caused Gabriel's forehead to bunch up.

"Text them to me," Gabriel insisted, and he clicked

the button to end the call. "The person who broke into your apartment left some pictures. Old ones from ten years ago."

Oh, God. "Not pictures of your parents' murders?"

He dragged in a long breath and nodded. "Brace yourself. Because the pictures are of you."

Chapter Eight

Gabriel was a thousand percent sure that it wasn't a good idea for Jodi to look at the pictures Jameson had just sent him. He was also equally certain that he wouldn't be able to stop her from seeing them. Not Jodi. She would insist on it.

From a law enforcement viewpoint, it was a good thing for her to study them. It might trigger some memories of the attack that would help them explain what was happening now. But it would also be an emotional nightmare for her. Something he wished he didn't have to put her through. Despite the thick wall Jodi had built around herself, Gabriel still wanted to protect her. Even when she wouldn't want him to do that.

He maximized the size of the first picture on his phone, but it still took Gabriel a few seconds to figure out exactly what he was seeing. It was a grainy shot, dark, but it soon became clear that it was of his front porch. The lights were on, and Jodi was in the doorway. She was wearing a familiar outfit—cutoff shorts and that red top.

Hell.

Someone had clicked a picture of them when Gabriel was turning her down, and while he didn't remember the exact words he'd said to her, the gist was for her to go back to his parents' house, where she was spending the night with Ivy.

"I didn't notice anyone," she said, her voice barely a whisper. She moved closer to him, arm to arm, and had another look.

He hadn't noticed anyone, either, but it could have been taken with a long-range lens. Still, if Gabriel had just glanced in that direction, he might have spotted the person and stopped what was about to happen.

But why would Travis have taken this?

The answer was—he wouldn't have. The man had been drunk, and it wasn't too likely he'd have been carrying a camera. Even if he'd used his phone for the shot, there was still no reason to do this. After all, Travis was well aware that Jodi often visited Ivy, and Gabriel.

Gabriel moved on to the next shot. This one was of Jodi walking away from his house. She was barely visible in the darkness, but she was already on the trail. Leaving. He was in the door, watching her go. He'd almost stopped her. Had almost run after her and kissed her. If he had, they wouldn't be standing here right now. Of course, his parents would likely still be dead since Gabriel had gotten the frantic call from Ivy less than five minutes after Jodi had left.

He cursed when he pulled up the third photo and tried to move his phone away so that Jodi wouldn't see it. Of course, she snatched it back and saw what had caused his profanity and had twisted his stomach into knots.

Jodi on the ground, bleeding out.

"The SOB took my picture while I was dying," she said.

Yeah, and that told him plenty that he hadn't known before. If Travis had indeed been the one to attack her because he'd thought she had witnessed the murders, he wouldn't have waited around to take a picture of her sliced up and on the ground. That applied to the other pictures, as well.

"You're right. Your father wouldn't have been the one to stab you," Gabriel admitted.

Jodi glanced at him and that's when Gabriel saw the tears in her eyes. She quickly blinked them away and turned her head.

"Yes." And that's all she said for several long seconds. "The person who took these photos was outside your house right about the time your parents were being killed." She paused. "My attack wasn't about them. It was about *me*."

The tears threatened again, and even though Gabriel figured it was a bad idea, he pulled her into his arms. He expected her to fight it or go stiff. But she didn't. Jodi melted against him.

That was what Gabriel wanted to protect her from seeing. Now, those images would stay with her just as they'd stayed with him. Because that's the way he'd seen her after he had found her just off the path.

"It wasn't my father," she whispered. Even through the emotion, he could hear the relief, and she looked up at him just as he looked down at her.

The air was already thick with emotion, but that eye-to-eye contact made it even worse. The attraction mixed with the old memories and the pain. Everything snowballed together until it felt as if he were being buried in an avalanche of heat. That's probably why he kissed her. Because it wasn't something he'd planned to do.

Definitely not a smart move.

His mouth barely touched hers before she scurried back as if he'd scalded her. "I'm sorry," he said at the exact moment that Jodi said, "I can't."

He nodded and then put even more distance between them. Gabriel was ready to close down the pictures so he could look at them later when Jodi wasn't around, but before he could do that, he heard the sound of a car pulling up in front of his house. Normally, that wouldn't have been a reason for concern, but there was nothing normal about what had been going on.

Gabriel drew his gun and went to the window just in time to see their visitor pull to a stop. It was a black SUV, and since the windows were heavily tinted, he couldn't see who was inside.

"Recognize that vehicle?" he asked Jodi.

"No." She'd drawn her gun as well, and even though she still had to be shaken from those photos, she wasn't showing any traces of being upset now. Like him, she was focused on a possible new threat.

Gabriel could see the front license plate of the SUV, and he was about to phone it in when someone stepped out.

Russell.

That didn't make Gabriel holster his gun, but it was obvious that Jodi and he weren't the only ones on edge. Russell glanced around while staying behind the cover of the SUV door. They were the kinds of glances a person would make if they thought someone was following them.

"Why the heck is he here?" Jodi grumbled.

Gabriel didn't know, but he was about to find out. He disarmed the security system so that it wouldn't go off when he opened the door, opening it about halfway.

"I have to talk to you." Russell ran onto the porch while still firing glances all around him.

Gabriel didn't back up. He certainly didn't invite

Russell inside, which earned him a puzzled look. "I'm in danger," the man added.

"Welcome to the club." But Gabriel knew he couldn't be flippant about this. He was a lawman. Danger came with the badge. Ditto for Jodi as a security specialist. But Russell was a businessman, a CPA, and this might be his first brush with some monster with a deadly agenda since he left the army.

Of course, in Gabriel's mind, Russell could be a suspect. Anyone with a personal connection to Jodi could be. Including Hector and August.

"Someone just tried to kill me," Russell spat out. He came closer as if ready to barge in, but Gabriel didn't let him.

Jodi, however, moved to Gabriel's side, which meant she was now in the possible line of fire if their bomber was still in the area. That was a good reason to put a quick end to this conversation so he could get her back inside.

Russell huffed. "Look, I just want you to put a stop to this. My wife and baby could be hurt."

Gabriel wanted to be unaffected by that, but he wasn't. He knew what it was like to have family members in danger. And what it was like to have that danger lead to their deaths.

"What happened?" Gabriel asked.

Russell looked around again and groaned softly. "I leave my car in the driveway overnight outside my house, and when I went to get in it early this morning, there were two rattlesnakes on the seats. Rattlesnakes!" he repeated like profanity. "What if my wife had gone out there with me to kiss me goodbye for work? She could have been killed."

Possibly. But since it was Russell's car, the snakes had been meant for him. "You didn't see anyone suspicious in the area?" Gabriel pressed. "And did you report it to SAPD?"

"Of course I reported it. I called them right away. They came and took my statement. They asked if I saw anyone, too, and I didn't. This has to stop," he repeated after another groan.

While still keeping watch of Russell, Gabriel took out his phone and made a quick call to Cameron to have him request a copy of Russell's incident report from SAPD.

"Maybe you can make a public statement," Russell went on, looking at Jodi now. "Or visit your father and make sure he's not behind this. He could have put his brother up to all this in order to clear his name, but I can't have my family at risk because of you."

Gabriel felt Jodi tense. Probably because those words would have felt like a slap to the face. But it was a strange way of putting it. Yes, Russell was upset, but why had he dumped all of this on Jodi?

"We have reason to believe that Travis wasn't the

one who attacked Jodi that night," Gabriel said, and he watched Russell's reaction.

And it was an interesting reaction all right. Russell's eyes widened, and he volleyed glances between Gabriel and her. "Then who the hell did it? Because that's probably the same SOB who put those snakes in my SUV."

Maybe. Probably, Gabriel amended. It was also likely the same person who'd blown up Jodi's car.

"You have to come up with a way to put an end to this," Russell went on, his voice more frantic now. "Maybe set a trap for him or something."

Gabriel had no plans to do that, especially since it would require using Jodi as bait, but he figured Jodi was already thinking of doing just that.

"I'm scared of Hector," Russell added. "If he's the one doing this, then he's got the people and the resources to hurt me and my family."

Gabriel hoped he didn't look too surprised at Russell's comment against Jodi's boss. Hector was indeed a possible suspect, but Russell made it seem as if adding the man to Gabriel's suspect list was a done deal.

"Why would you think Hector's behind this?" Jodi asked, taking the question right out of Gabriel's mouth.

Russell lifted his shoulder. "I thought it was obvious. The guy's crazy in love with you. And he can't be happy that you're staying here with Gabriel.

Something like that might send Hector off the deep end. Heck, it might send August off the deep end, too." He settled his attention on Gabriel. "August really hates you, and he wouldn't want his niece spending time with the man who helped put his brother in prison."

August did feel that way, but Gabriel decided not to confirm it. He just waited to see if Russell would say anything else. He didn't.

Russell checked his watch. "I need to be getting to work." He started to leave but then turned back. "I don't want you calling my home or going there. It'd only upset my wife even more." He wasn't talking to Gabriel but rather Jodi.

"No worries. I won't go there." Her voice was tight enough for Gabriel to know that she wasn't pleased with what was essentially a dig. It was long over between Jodi and Russell, and Gabriel doubted she had feelings for the man, but maybe Russell thought she did.

Gabriel stepped back so he could shut the door. He also made another call to Cameron, and the deputy answered on the first ring.

"I need you to bring in Hector and August for questioning again—" Gabriel started.

"August is already here," Cameron interrupted. "And he's demanding to speak to you."

"Put him on the phone." Gabriel still wanted to

do a face-to-face interview with both men, but he could possibly clear up some things right now. Well, one thing anyway. "While I'm talking to him, see if you can pull up any financials on Hector, Russell and August. The FBI should have already done that because of the investigation into the email threats and the latest murder."

"Will do. Oh, and brace yourself because August is mad." There was sarcasm dripping from Cameron's voice, probably because August was usually angry about something.

"Where are you?" August snapped the moment he came on the line. "And where's my niece?"

"We're both safe," Gabriel answered. Even though August likely knew Jodi was at the ranch, he didn't want to confirm it. "I just got a visit from Russell. Any chance you put some snakes in his car?"

"What?" August howled. "Is that what he said?" He didn't pause long enough for Gabriel to respond. "Because he's a bald-faced liar. I hope you asked him if he's the one who killed your folks and knifed Jodi."

He hadn't, but Gabriel wasn't planning to accuse Russell of anything yet, especially since he didn't have any evidence.

"Russell had an alibi for the night of the attacks," Gabriel reminded him.

"Yeah, so what? It was a girl he'd met at a bar who admitted she'd been drinking. She could have passed out and not even known he'd gone out and done something like that."

Gabriel hadn't intended for the conversation to swing in this direction, but he went with it. "Okay, I'll bite. What motive would Russell have to kill my folks? He didn't even know them."

Of course, Gabriel had a theory that could work—that Russell could have killed them after going to the house to look for Jodi. Collateral damage.

"Russell didn't have to know them to kill them," August pointed out. "Maybe he was tanked up on drugs. Maybe he just wanted to kill something or somebody, and they were the ones who drew the short straw. I'm just saying, you need to take a hard look at that liar. If there were snakes in his car, he might have put them there himself."

Yes, and that's why Gabriel wanted to read the report from SAPD. There might be something suspicious that stood out. Also, Gabriel could start calling around to the local snake handlers to see if anyone had purchased any recently. Some people collected them for their venom and just because they liked having dangerous "pets." If any of them had recently sold a pair of snakes, it could lead them to Russell.

"Are you going to ask Hector if he put snakes in that idiot's car?" August went on.

"You bet I will. Now, wait there until I can get

into the office and we can have a longer chat. For now, give the phone back to Cameron."

"He's on the other line, but I'll put the phone on his desk."

From the sound of it, August practically threw it there. He obviously wasn't happy about having to wait on Gabriel, but people often said more when they were riled, so he'd let August stew a while longer.

Then, he could figure out what to do about Jodi.

"I could go to the sheriff's office with you," she offered while he waited for Cameron. "If you give me access to a computer and a phone, I can start trying to take a better look at the photos that the intruder left at my apartment. I might see something I hadn't noticed before."

That was what Gabriel was afraid of. Still, the killer and she were likely the only ones at that particular time on the part of the trail where she'd been attacked that night. So Jodi might indeed see something new.

Along with having a panic attack.

But that was a bridge he'd cross if they got to it.

"Sorry about the wait," Cameron said when he came back. "I've got something to tell you, but I want to do that in your office. I'm walking there right now."

The deputy probably wanted some privacy because August was right there in his face, but it meant waiting a couple of seconds. "It's about Russell," Cameron said when he finally continued. "The FBI has been monitoring him along with Jodi, you and anyone else who might be connected to the recent threats, and they might have found something."

Jodi moved closer to him, clearly trying to hear what Cameron was saying, so Gabriel put the call on speaker. "Jodi's listening," Gabriel warned the deputy. That way, Cameron could tone down anything that might be disturbing to her.

"Russell recently withdrew a rather large sum of money in cash. Nine grand. It came from an account he had before he got married. His wife's name isn't on the account. She might not even know it exists."

Not telling a spouse about an account wasn't unheard of, but that wasn't what caught Gabriel's attention. It was the amount of money. Just enough not to attract suspicion. At least it wouldn't have been if Russell weren't being monitored. Nine thousand was enough to pay off Billy and hire the guy who'd broken into Jodi's apartment. Maybe even enough to pay the man who'd blown up her car.

When Gabriel's eyes met Jodi's, he realized she'd come to the same conclusion.

"Does the FBI have any idea what Russell used the money for?" Gabriel asked Cameron.

"Not yet. He didn't deposit it into another account,

didn't get a cashier's check with it, either. You want me to get him in here and question him?"

"No. Check with the FBI. It's possible they'll want to monitor him to see if this has anything to do with the murder or anything else."

"Yeah, about that," Cameron continued. "The lab got an ID on the dead guy. It's not good, Gabriel." He paused. "The guy was a cop."

Chapter Nine

Jodi's mind was whirling with everything Gabriel and she had learned. Whirling, too, because she'd been on edge the entire drive from his ranch to the sheriff's office. It wasn't far, less than ten miles, but each moment they'd been on the road had felt like an eternity.

Once Cameron had told Gabriel that their dead guy was a cop, Gabriel hadn't asked anything else. He'd just told the deputy that they were on their way there. Not just to read the reports on Russell but also so that Gabriel could reinterview August and Hector.

"I don't want you near the windows," Gabriel told her when he rushed her inside the building.

Cameron was right there to hand him some papers, but Gabriel paused only long enough to take them, and then he led her to his office. He lowered the blinds on the single window behind his desk and waited for Cameron to come in.

"That's a copy of the police report that Russell filed about those snakes," Cameron explained. "We're coming up empty on who might have gotten the snakes, but we'll keep looking. The next paper is about our dead guy. His name was Calvin Lasher, a small-town cop from Louisiana who'd recently been reported missing. I don't know why his prints weren't in the system, but it could have been some kind of computer error."

Jodi repeated the man's name, but it didn't mean anything to her. "Why was he here in Blue River?" She went to Gabriel's side and started reading through the initial report that Cameron had done on the dead man.

"I don't have a clue," Cameron answered. "Lasher's boss and family don't know, either, but his boss said he'd been investigating Hector."

That caused both Gabriel and her to take their attention from the paper and look at Cameron. "Why?" they said in unison.

"An illegal wiretap. Lasher had arrested a pimp who wanted a plea deal. The pimp said Hector had set up an illegal tap on his phone."

Gabriel turned to her. "You know anything about that?"

"No. But we do have out-of-state clients. It's possible Hector knew one of this pimp's girls, and maybe she had complained to him."

"It's not as if Hector hasn't done something like this before," Gabriel grumbled.

She didn't miss the disdain in Gabriel's voice. "True, but it would have been stupid for him to do it when he's on probation. Something like this could land him in jail."

Of course, that might not have stopped Hector. His favorite saying was, never mistake the law for justice, so he was always bending rules to the point of breaking them.

"Hector doesn't live in Blue River, either," she added. "Seems a stretch that he could have lured a cop to the Beckett ranch in order to kill him."

"A stretch but not impossible," Gabriel pointed out. "This way he could eliminate someone who might be able to put him back behind bars."

Maybe. But that seemed extreme for what would have turned out to be a fairly short jail sentence, and it was a sentence that Hector could have perhaps beaten. He had a knack for escaping time behind bars.

"When did this wiretap supposedly happen?" she asked Cameron.

"About two weeks ago."

"Good, that's recent enough that the file won't be archived yet," Jodi explained. "If you let me use your computer, I'll see if I can access the info."

Gabriel motioned for her to use the laptop on his desk, and she was about to log on to the Sentry page when she heard footsteps in the hall. Cameron and Gabriel immediately reacted, both of them putting their hands over their weapons, but she saw them relax just as fast.

"Is my sister here?" someone demanded.

Theo.

Jodi hurried out from behind the desk to see her brother walking up the hall. It was the first time she'd seen him in a year, and she went to him, wanting to hug him but not sure how he would react.

Once Theo and she had been so close. But that had changed the night of her attack. In the aftermath, each of them had been dealing with their own pain. She, because she had nearly died, and Theo, because he'd been a suspect in the murders.

He'd changed a lot since she'd seen him. His hair was long, practically to his shoulders, and he was dressed more like a cowboy-biker than a federal agent. She didn't know if his leather vest and rodeo buckle were his own clothes or if this was something he'd been wearing undercover.

"Jodi," he greeted. He lifted his hand as if he might reach out for her, but he didn't. Maybe because he saw the unease in her eyes. Of course, there was plenty of unease in his eyes, as well. Probably because there was no love lost between Gabriel, Cameron and him.

She didn't ask him where he'd been. Jodi knew as a deep cover DEA agent Theo wouldn't be able to tell her anyway. Plus, she wasn't sure she wanted to know the kind of danger he was in on a daily basis.

It was already hard enough to accept that he might never be a real part of her life.

Equally hard to accept that both of them wanted it that way.

"Are you okay?" Theo said to her.

She nodded. "You?"

He lifted his shoulder. "I got a threat just like all of you, but it's been sitting on my old server for days, so I just now got word of it." Theo turned his attention to Gabriel. "I'm guessing Ivy got one, too?"

It wasn't a surprise that Theo had asked about Gabriel's sister, Ivy. Theo and she been a couple of steps past just being close.

"Yeah, Ivy got one all right, but she's not here," Gabriel answered. Cameron and he shared a glance. "In fact, Ivy doesn't stay in touch with us."

Yet another casualty of the aftermath of that horrible night. Gabriel's family had been torn apart as well, and Jodi suspected that Ivy just hadn't been able to stay in Blue River with the god-awful memories of the place.

"I heard about the recent attack," Theo went on. "And the dead cop. I can't stay, but I wanted to let you know that I made some calls to a few criminal informants to see if there's any buzz about this. There isn't," he added a heartbeat later. "But I did turn up something that's been bothering me. It's about Russell."

Of course, Russell was on their suspect radar, but

it was still a surprise to hear Theo bring up his name. "You talked to Russell?" she asked, ready to tell him about the rattlesnake incident. But Theo continued before she could do that.

"I didn't talk to him, but a CI happened to know one of his old friends. According to the guy, Russell was binge drinking after Jodi broke up with him. He possibly even used drugs. The friend said Russell kept going on and on about Jodi leaving him for some deputy."

Gabriel.

"I never mentioned Gabriel's name to Russell," she explained, "and I certainly never told Russell I was leaving him for Gabriel."

"The friend said Russell figured it out when he heard you talking with Ivy." Theo paused, rubbed his fingers over his left eyebrow. "From the part of the conversation he listened to, Russell decided that you were going to try to seduce Gabriel."

That had been the plan. No need to verify it because it was part of the statement she'd given the cops after the attack. Of course, Russell wouldn't have had access to the report to confirm his suspicions, but that sort of info tended to get out.

"Russell didn't say anything to you about eavesdropping on your conversation with Ivy?" Gabriel asked her.

"No. And he didn't say anything to the cops about it, either." Unlike Russell, she had managed to get her hands on the report and had read every word of Russell's statement.

"Who are you looking at for these latest attacks?" Theo asked Gabriel.

"We have someone, a schizophrenic teenager, in lockup at a mental hospital." Gabriel made a sound of dismissal that Theo echoed. "That brings us to Hector March, your uncle August and Russell. We already know Russell had a thin alibi for that night. And he came here yesterday to Blue River, maybe hoping to see Jodi." A muscle flickered in Gabriel's jaw. "Jodi put out the word that she was remembering details of her attack."

Theo cursed. "Why the hell would you do that?"

She should have thought before she reacted, but Jodi lifted her T-shirt to remind him of the scars. Even though she only uncovered her stomach, there was plenty enough to see there.

Theo cursed again and glanced away. "Those scars are the very reason you shouldn't have put out a lure like that," he said. But he dismissed it with a shake of his head. "If I'd been in your position, I would have done the same thing. That's not a seal of approval, by the way, since most people think I'm crazy for doing what I do." He snapped toward Gabriel. "You can protect her?"

"I'll try."

"I'm trained to protect myself," she reminded both of them, but she might as well have been talking to the air because Gabriel and Theo stared at each other, some man-bond thing going on between them.

"Whoever attacked you outsized you by a good five inches," Gabriel said. "Outweighed you, too. We know that from the angle of your wounds and placement of your bruises. And all the training in the world won't stop him from trying to put a bullet in you."

Theo seemed pleased with Gabriel's stance. And the truth was—so was she. Even though it felt like this battle was hers and hers alone, it wasn't. In fact, her attacker could use Gabriel, Cameron or even Theo to get to her. That didn't make this easier to accept.

Especially not with this heat swirling between Gabriel and her.

The heat couldn't lead to anything, but her body was having trouble remembering that. And it was getting in the way of what she needed to be focusing on—the person who wanted her dead.

"If Hector's behind this," Theo went on, "things could get uglier than they already are. And as for August, well, he could just hire enough guns to finish whatever the hell he wants finished. Either way, be careful."

She would, but it sickened her to think that it might be any of those men. At various times in her life, she'd trusted each one of them. Of course, it could always be someone else. A nutjob whose name they didn't even know.

Not exactly a thought to ease her churning stomach.

"I have to go," Theo said, not sounding very pleased about that. "If anyone asks, I wasn't here. I can't give you a phone number, and you can't try to contact me," he added to Jodi, "but if I hear anything that'll help catch this piece of dirt, I'll find a way to get the info to you."

Jodi was about to thank Theo, but before she could do that, he brushed a kiss on her cheek, causing her to go board stiff. Theo noticed, too. He pulled back, making eye contact with her, and even though he didn't curse out loud again, she thought that might be what he was doing in his head.

"We'll talk soon," Theo whispered, and just like that she was a little kid again and he was her big brother. All the tension vanished. It wouldn't last, of course. Wounds this deep didn't heal, but for a moment it was good to have Theo back.

She stood there, watching him walk away until he disappeared out the door. Jodi turned to go to Gabriel's computer so she could do the search on the Sentry files, but Gabriel stepped in front of her as soon as she was back in his office. He shot Cameron a glance, and the deputy mumbled something about needing to check on a report.

Uh-oh.

That was not a good look in Gabriel's eyes, especially since his gaze kept drifting toward her stomach. "That's the first time I've seen your scars," he said.

"Sorry."

"Don't be." He put his fingers under her chin, barely touching her, but lifted it so they were staring at each other. "Please tell me you've let a man kiss you in the past ten years."

She shook her head, moving away from him. Not because his touch had sent her into a panic.

But because it *hadn't* done that.

No way did she want to talk about this with Gabriel, especially with all this energy and attraction zinging between them. While part of her desperately wanted a kiss from Gabriel, it would open wounds she didn't want reopened.

"The Sentry files," Jodi said once she'd gathered enough breath to speak. Somehow, she managed enough energy, too, to move away from him. Definitely not easy.

"You do know that by not answering," he grumbled, "that it was an answer."

Yes. She hadn't let a man kiss her since the attack. Hadn't even wanted a man to do that.

Until now.

Mercy, she was in trouble.

Jodi forced her attention on the laptop. Work had always gotten her mind off things, and she needed that to happen now. It did. The moment she accessed the files, she started going through them, looking for any of Hector's active cases. There were at least a dozen, and none of them had anything to do with their dead guy, Calvin Lasher. In fact, none of them were cases that involved pimps or eavesdropping devices.

She shook her head and was able to move to the archives when she spotted something. Not a case assigned to Hector but to her.

"I didn't work on this," Jodi mumbled, scrolling through it. "But it did involve a prostitute from the New Orleans area. Her name was Kitty Martin, and she wanted to hire Sentry for bodyguard duty."

"About how much would it have cost for that?" Gabriel asked after a long pause. Obviously, he'd been reading the file from over her shoulder.

"Hundreds at least. There's a start date of a month ago with no completion date. If she'd actually hired me for the full month, the cost would have been in the thousands." She shrugged. "Maybe Hector intended to assign the case to me but took it himself. Or else Ms. Martin changed her mind about wanting our services."

If either of those things had happened, then it should have been in the file and under Hector's name, not hers. Plus, there was the part about the dead cop who'd been investigating Hector's involvement with a pimp from New Orleans. Jodi doubted that was a coincidence.

And apparently Gabriel thought so, too. Mumbling some profanity, he took out his phone. "I'm putting out an APB on Hector. I want him brought in immediately."

Chapter Ten

Gabriel didn't like the way this investigation was going. Somehow, he needed to figure out who was behind the recent attack so he could stop another one. Because he doubted the danger was over.

Neither was the fallout.

Jodi was pacing again, something she'd been doing for the past three hours while they waited for SAPD to find Hector and bring him in. While it seemed as if seeing her brother had soothed her a bit, that soothing was long gone now. Probably because she dreaded the idea of Hector being guilty. It would mean the only man she'd completely trusted for the past ten years hadn't been someone she could trust after all.

There was a knock at his office door, causing Jodi to whirl in that direction. Gabriel could see her steeling herself up. But it wasn't necessary because it was only Cameron.

"It'll be another half hour or so before Hector gets

here," Cameron told them right off, "but I finally got permission for an interview with Billy Coleman."

That was good news. Or at least it would be if Billy wasn't so drugged up that he couldn't talk to them. Still, it was a start.

"You want me to go see Billy, or should I stay here and do the interview with Hector?" Cameron asked.

If Gabriel could have been in two places, that would be ideal, but he needed to stay put with Jodi. "Since Jameson's already in San Antonio today at the Rangers' office, have him go see Billy," Gabriel instructed. "Jameson can probably be there in a matter of minutes. I also want him to record the interview if he can." Though he seriously doubted Billy's doctors were going to allow that.

Cameron nodded, looked at Jodi. "This probably won't come as a surprise, but Hector's not happy about having to come in."

"No. I wouldn't imagine he would be." Jodi paused. "Did he say anything about me?"

"Words that you probably don't want to hear. The man has a temper."

Great. Not a good combination, and when Hector aimed his temper and venom at Jodi, it would eat away at her.

"Anything else in the Sentry computer files?" Cameron asked, motioning to the computer that was still on Gabriel's desk.

Jodi shook her head. "And I've been through

every one of them for the past year. Those the year of the attack, too."

Cameron's eyebrow lifted, and he shifted his attention back to Gabriel. "You don't think Hector's connected to your mom and dad?"

Gabriel blew out a weary breath. "If he is, he didn't surface as a suspect."

"And I didn't know him back then," Jodi added. She was no doubt thinking about how Hector just showed up out of the blue in her hospital room. "So, unless Hector's somehow linked to the late Hattie Osmond and that money she was seemingly paying out, then he wouldn't have had any part in the murder of Gabriel's parents."

But maybe he had a part now. Hector could have killed the cop and now could be so jealous of Jodi's return to Blue River that he could want her punished. Or worse.

"Would Hector have even been old enough to be swindling money from Hattie?" Cameron, again.

"He would have been in his early twenties," Gabriel supplied. "And he got his money to open Sentry from somewhere." Of course, it was a stretch to believe the money had come from Hattie, but Gabriel had to look at all the angles.

That angle included the most recent ones. The ones that included Jodi's uncle.

"Go ahead and call August and bring him back in for questioning, too. We know that Russell recently withdrew some money from his accounts, but maybe August did, as well."

Cameron nodded, turned to leave but then stopped. He eyed both Jodi and him. "If you want to take turns guarding Jodi, just let me know."

"What was that about?" Jodi asked the moment Cameron was out of the room.

Gabriel scowled and shut the door.

"Oh," she said, obviously picking up on the emotions behind his scowl. "He thinks we're getting together. Cameron clearly doesn't know me," she added in a mumble.

Gabriel hadn't needed a reminder of his earlier conversation with Jodi, the one about kissing, but her mumble brought it back to the surface anyway. He probably should just let it go, but it was hard to do. Plenty of things were hard when it came to Jodi.

He went to her, knowing it was a mistake but not able to stop himself, either. He cursed this attraction that seemed to be growing by leaps and bounds. The timing for it sucked, and plain and simple, it could be dangerous.

But this wasn't about common sense.

"You're feeling guilty," she said out of the blue. "If you'd kissed me that night, or had sex with me, then I wouldn't be like this."

Since it was true, Gabriel didn't deny it. But there was a flip side to this. "If you'd stayed and we'd had sex, it might not have turned out so well." Of course, almost anything would have been better than what Jodi had endured.

"Yeah. We're back to *sex is a commitment* when both of us know that for you it wasn't."

Gabriel tried to tamp down the slam of emotion that caused inside him. "Sex *with you* would have been a commitment."

As soon as he said the words, he knew it was a mistake. A mistake because it was the truth, and in this case he was pretty sure the truth wasn't going to help.

It didn't.

She looked at him, shook her head as if that couldn't possibly be right and then she cursed. Gabriel knew how she felt. He wanted to curse, too. But instead he made the mistake much, much worse by taking hold of her hand.

He didn't jump into a kiss. Though that's exactly what he wanted to do. Gabriel gave her a moment to adjust to his touching her. Gave her another moment while he eased her closer to him.

"I thought you hated me," she said.

"I wanted to hate you," he admitted. "But mostly I just wanted you. And you were too young. It wouldn't have taken you long to start resenting that you weren't out having those life experiences you should have been having."

The corner of her mouth quivered with a half

smile, but it wasn't a smile of humor. "So much for life experiences."

Yeah. The attack had rid her of that chance. And even though it wasn't fair, now wasn't the time to go back and re-create the kiss he'd wanted to give her that night. This was the time to focus on the investigation so he could stop another attack.

But he didn't do that.

While he still had hold of her hand, he leaned in and brushed his mouth over hers. It barely qualified as a kiss, but it slammed into him like a Mack truck. It apparently did some slamming into Jodi, too, because she made a sound that was like a gasp.

Gabriel pulled back to make sure she wasn't on the verge of a panic attack. She wasn't. That wasn't panic he saw in her eyes. It was the fire from this blasted attraction.

She didn't move closer to him. Didn't touch him. Both cues that he should just back away, but again he didn't. Gabriel slid his arm around her waist, pulled her to him and kissed her.

Jodi went stiff. At first. Then, the stiffness vanished when she moved into the kiss. Of course, that meant her moving against him, too. Specifically, her breasts against his chest. Normally, it wouldn't have been a turn-on to be kissing a woman who was plenty unsure about this, but it fired every part of his body.

Especially one part that shouldn't be fired.

She tasted exactly how he thought she would. Like something special—a mixture of fire and innocence. He forced himself to remember that it wasn't a good combination. Of course, there was little about this that was good, other than the kiss itself. And that silky moan of pleasure that purred in her throat.

Kissing Jodi was one thing, but that was as far as it could go. Because that old rule still applied here. Sex with her would still be a commitment, and there was no way either of them was in a place for that to happen. That's why Gabriel moved back from her.

"Any feelings of a panic attack?" he asked.

She hesitated a moment, as if trying to figure that out, and shook her head. "Too bad, huh? Because a panic attack would have kept us away from each other."

Jodi was right about that. "It's still not a good idea for us to be kissing…or anything else."

No hesitation that time. She quickly nodded, but then ran her tongue on her bottom lip. She probably hadn't meant it to be sexual, but it certainly felt that way to his body, which was primed and ready to go. Gabriel had to remind his body that it wasn't going to get Jodi.

"But at least now I know," she said. She lifted her shoulder when he stared at her. "Before I was attacked, I thought a lot about kissing you. Now, I can tick that experience off my bucket list."

Yeah, but he was betting her bucket list didn't include dealing with the flames that kiss had fanned inside them.

"Sheriff Beckett?" someone called out. Except it was more of a shout. And Gabriel knew that voice belonged to Hector.

Cameron had been right about Hector not being pleased because when Gabriel opened the door and spotted him, he could see Hector's eyes were narrowed to slits. The narrowing didn't ease up when Hector shifted his attention to Jodi.

"Why the hell did you let him do this?" Hector snarled to her.

Gabriel figured he was the *him* in that question. He also guessed that the guy in the suit next to Hector was his lawyer. The two uniformed SAPD officers behind them signed off on some paperwork that Cameron gave them and headed out—fast. No doubt because it had not been a pleasant ride with Hector to the sheriff's office, and they were eager to get away from him.

"We need you here to answer some questions," Jodi explained to her very riled boss.

"You didn't need the cops for that. I would have come. All you had to do was call and ask."

Gabriel was betting Hector wouldn't have been so cooperative if anyone but Jodi had made that call. And he wouldn't be so cooperative now, either. Clearly, Hector saw this as a betrayal on Jodi's part, and Gabriel hoped that didn't come back to haunt them.

"You have no grounds to hold my client," the suit snapped.

"Yes, I do." Gabriel motioned for them to follow him into an interview room. "He's connected to the man who was murdered. A cop named Calvin Lasher. Want to tell me about him?" he added once Hector, the lawyer and Gabriel were inside. Jodi stayed in the doorway. Maybe because she knew this was an official interview, and she didn't want to do anything to compromise it.

But it was Hector who waved her in. "You honestly believe I had something to do with a dead cop?"

"Lasher was investigating you," Jodi answered.

If looks could have killed, Hector would have finished Jodi off then and there. Yeah, he definitely saw this as a betrayal, so Gabriel tried to put the focus back on himself.

"Lasher thought you'd broken the law," Gabriel told him. "And since we know you've done that in the past—"

"Don't finish that," Hector warned him. "I didn't do anything wrong." He stopped, huffed, and it seemed to Gabriel that he was trying to rein in his temper. "About a month ago, I got a call from a woman, Kitty Martin. She thought maybe her pimp was bringing in underage girls that he was luring in with drugs. She wanted to go to the cops, but her pimp was violent, and she thought he might kill her."

That all meshed with what they'd learned, but there were still some gaps in the information. "Lasher thought you'd done an illegal wiretap on the pimp."

Hector was shaking his head before Gabriel even finished. "I had him under surveillance, but that was it. Then, I got a call from Kitty, and she told me to back off, that she didn't want to pursue the case. So, I stopped."

Gabriel couldn't tell if Hector was lying about that or not, and judging from the sound Jodi made, she was in the same boat. "Why put the file under my name?" she asked.

Hector's eyes widened for a moment. Either he was surprised or pretending to be. "Must have been a clerical error. I didn't do it," he added when Jodi and Gabriel just stared at him. He cursed. "If I'd wanted to cover up an involvement in this, why would I have left Kitty's file in the Sentry database?"

"Maybe an oversight on your part," Gabriel readily answered. That earned him a glare from both Hector and his attorney.

"I didn't do anything wrong," Hector repeated, turning that glare on Jodi. "I was just trying to help a woman, the same way I tried to help you ten years ago."

Jodi glanced away, and she said some profanity

under her breath. "I will always be thankful for what you did for me," she added, "but Gabriel and I need answers."

"You mean you want to send me to jail," Hector snarled.

"No," Jodi readily argued. "I just want the danger to stop." She paused. "Is it possible that Kitty was setting you up in some way?" Jodi looked at Gabriel to finish that. "Maybe someone posing as a prostitute did this, so they could kill a cop and put the blame on Hector?"

It was a theory. Not necessarily a good one, but Gabriel thought about it for a moment. If this was a copycat killing to clear Travis's name, it didn't make sense to frame Hector. Especially since Hector didn't have an obvious connection to those decade-old crimes. A copycat would have stood a better chance of framing Russell or August.

Of course, maybe Russell or August were behind this.

So, perhaps this was as Jodi had suggested and was simply about getting rid of a cop. Someone other than Hector could have had it out for Lasher. Someone who could have seen Hector as an easy target since he had a police record and maybe the wrong enemy who wanted to eliminate both Lasher and Hector. It was certainly something Hector's lawyer would argue.

And a judge would agree.

Now, Gabriel cursed because that meant he couldn't hold Hector. No way would the charges stick unless he had more evidence. Which he didn't.

Hector smiled as if he knew exactly what conclusion Gabriel had just reached.

"Jodi's in danger," Gabriel reminded the man. That caused Hector's smile to vanish. "I need you to go through all your files and figure out if someone is indeed setting you up. Find me anyone connected to Lasher and you."

Hector nodded, but he still looked riled to the core when he stood and faced Jodi. "So, you're helping Gabriel now?" he asked.

She shrugged. "He and I are in the same proverbial boat."

Hector shifted his gaze to Gabriel, and like before, it seemed as if the man could sense what was going on in Gabriel's head. And what was going on was the very recent memory of kissing Jodi.

"Do you know anything about rattlesnakes being put in Russell Laney's car?" Gabriel asked, and he watched the man's expression.

Surprise followed by annoyance went through Hector's eyes. "Trying to pin something else on me?"

"Just asking. And waiting for an answer."

"No, I didn't," Hector insisted. "That sounds like something a coward would do. I'm not a coward."

He probably wasn't, but that didn't mean Hector hadn't resorted to this low level of intimidation.

"Is my client free to go?" the lawyer asked.

Gabriel took his time nodding and wished that it didn't have to be this way. He wanted to get at least one of their suspects off the street, but apparently that wasn't going to happen today.

Jodi stepped back into the hall so that Hector could leave. The man walked out, shooting her a warning glance from over his shoulder, and his lawyer and he finally left the building. The moment they were outside, Cameron came to them.

"I didn't want to say anything with them here," Cameron started, "but I might have something. I called the prison to see who'd visited Jodi's father in the last month, and an interesting name popped up. Russell. He was there the day before we found Lasher's body."

Well, hell. This might be exactly the connection Gabriel had been looking for.

"I've already got approval from the warden if you want to visit Travis," Cameron added.

"I do," Jodi and Gabriel said in unison.

Since Gabriel doubted there was anything he could say or do to stop her from going with him on this visit, he just motioned for Cameron to follow them.

"Pull the cruiser to the front," he instructed Cameron, "so that Jodi won't have to be outside for very long."

Cameron nodded and headed out.

"You don't have to see your father if you don't want to," Gabriel offered her.

"No. I'm going."

That's exactly what he figured she would say. "How long has it been since you've seen him?"

"Shortly after his conviction eight and a half years ago." She paused. "The last visit didn't go well." Another pause. "He broke down, apologizing for nearly killing me."

That got his attention. "I thought he didn't remember anything about the attacks?"

She blew out a long, weary breath. "He didn't. But after sitting through all the court testimony, he had to consider that he could have possibly done it." She dismissed it with the wave of her hand. "My father is a broken man. I think he would have apologized for anything at that point, and he told me then not to come back. He didn't want me to see him behind bars."

Which would make this visit hard on Travis as well as Jodi. Of course, Gabriel didn't care a rat how Travis felt. He only hoped this wasn't a wasted trip.

The moment that Cameron pulled to a stop in front of the building, Gabriel got Jodi moving. He threw open the back door of the cruiser so she could climb inside, and he quickly followed behind her. However, the moment Cameron drove off, Gabriel's phone rang, and when he saw Jameson's name on the screen, he answered it right away. Since this was almost certainly about Billy, he put the call on speaker so that Jodi and Cameron could hear.

"It was no-go on recording the chat with Billy," Jameson said right off. "Our chat, if you can call it that, only lasted a few minutes. And his attorney and two doctors were there the whole time. Added to that, Billy was higher than a kite."

Gabriel didn't bother groaning since he hadn't expected much to come of it anyway. That's why Jameson surprised him with what he said next.

"Billy kept mentioning rattlesnakes," Jameson continued. "In fact, at first that's all he said while he rocked back and forth and asked for his mommy."

Jodi touched her fingers to her mouth, shook her head. They hadn't needed any other proof that they were dealing with a troubled teenager, but there it was.

"And then as I was leaving," Jameson went on, "Billy said a name. Not Russell. But August."

"Did he connect August to the snakes?" Jodi jumped to ask.

"No. But Billy did say I should watch out or that Uncle August would kill me. Then, he said ''bye, Jodi.'"

Jodi. Maybe he'd said that because August had mentioned her to Billy. Or it could simply be something Billy had overheard while he was at the sheriff's office.

"Please tell me you found some kind of link between Billy and August," Gabriel said while he kept watch around them. He didn't breathe easier until they were clear of all the buildings on Main Street.

"Not yet. But someone must have told Billy about those rattlesnakes because he was locked up when it happened."

Maybe he'd heard it from the person who'd killed, or who'd put him up to killing, Lasher. But that didn't mean the person was August. As much as it pained Gabriel to admit it, someone could have planted that name in Billy's sick mind. Heck, planted the idea of rattlesnakes, too.

"Jodi and I are going to the jail now to see Travis," Gabriel told his brother, "but when I get back, I'll question August again."

"I can do it. I'm heading back to Blue River right now, and I can call him on the way and have him meet me."

"Thanks." As much as Gabriel wanted to hear what Jodi's uncle had to say, he was already bone tired, and he had to face Travis. Besides, any confrontation with August would include Jodi as well, and Gabriel doubted that she wanted to deal with him, either.

Gabriel ended the call and was putting his phone in his pocket when he glanced at the road ahead. They were still several miles from the interstate and were on a two-lane country road where there was usually little traffic. If this had been normal circumstances, the car ahead of them wouldn't have caught his eye. But since things lately had been far from normal, Gabriel had a closer look.

It was a dark blue four-door, and the driver turned on the right blinker before he pulled onto the shoulder. Such that it was. It was really just a narrow strip of gravel that divided the farm road from a ditch.

"You think that could be trouble?" Cameron asked.

"Maybe." And just in case it was, Gabriel added to Jodi, "Get down on the seat." Thankfully, she didn't argue, but she did draw her sidearm. So did Gabriel. "Don't stop or slow down," he added to Cameron.

Cameron didn't, but as soon as they got closer to the car, Gabriel saw that the driver's-side window was down.

And that the driver was wearing a ski mask.

Before Gabriel could even react, the ski-masked thug fired a shot directly into the cruiser.

Chapter Eleven

Jodi didn't see the gunman, but she instantly knew that someone had fired a shot. The sound of it blasted through the air and slammed into the window on the front passenger's side of the cruiser. The glass cracked, but it held, thank God.

She lifted her head to see what was going on, but Gabriel pushed her right back down. However, she did get a glimpse of a man behind the wheel of the car. Since he had a gun in his hand, he was almost certainly the one who'd shot at them.

When he fired two more rounds at them, Jodi had her answer.

"Get us out of here," Gabriel told Cameron.

Cameron did, but Jodi also heard another sound. The squeal of tires from the car that was now behind them. It was coming after them.

Gabriel cursed. "There are at least two of them." One to drive and one to shoot, and that's exactly what was happening.

The bullets continued to slam into the cruiser. So far, the metal and glass were holding, but eventually the shots could make it through. Worse, Cameron couldn't get away from the bullets by going on the interstate. Because there'd be plenty of other vehicles, and an innocent bystander could be killed. Of course, the same could happen if one of the ranchers who lived out this way was on the road at the wrong time.

Gabriel took out his phone, and while she couldn't hear the other end of the conversation, he asked for backup and gave them their location. It wouldn't be long before one of the deputies arrived, and maybe another cruiser could come up behind the car, and they could sandwich in the shooters.

"I want at least one of these clowns alive," Gabriel said under his breath.

Jodi wanted the same thing. Because then they might find out who was behind this. Heck, they might even be able to confront the person directly since it could be any one of their three suspects in that car.

"Hell," Cameron said. He didn't hit the brakes, but he did slow down.

That caused Jodi to peer over the seat again. One look and Jodi was doing some cursing, too. Because straight ahead, sideways on the road, was another car.

Jodi doubted it was a coincidence. And it wasn't.

Because almost immediately someone from inside that vehicle started shooting at them.

"I can't get around the car," Cameron said, slowing down even more.

Again, that wasn't a coincidence. So, they'd either have to stop and be sitting ducks caught in cross fire or crash into the car with the hopes of taking out that set of gunmen while not disabling the cruiser.

Not exactly stellar options.

Gabriel glanced at her. "There's not a ranch trail we can use," he let her know.

The gunmen probably knew that, too. And that meant Cameron, Gabriel and she were going to have to fight their way out of this. It wasn't the first time Jodi had been caught in gunfire. There'd been two cases where someone had tried to kill people she'd been assigned to protect. Like those other times, there was no feeling of panic. Strange, but in some ways this felt more comfortable than having someone touch her.

"I'll keep an eye on the guys behind us," she offered, and Gabriel didn't decline. Probably because he knew it would no longer do any good for her to stay down. The closer they got to the second car, the more bullets riddled the cruiser.

Cameron cursed when one of the shots tore through the front windshield. It was just a matter of time before more made it into the interior, and that meant they had to do something fast.

"Slow down enough to minimize the impact for us," Gabriel instructed. "But ram the cruiser right into the shooter."

The shooter wasn't hard to see because he was leaning out of the passenger's side of the second car. "I might be able to take him out," Jodi said. "I'm a good shot."

For a moment she thought Gabriel was about to agree to that, but two more shots tore through the glass, one in the front and one in the rear.

"Hit the second car!" Gabriel told Cameron. He pushed Jodi back down, but both knew she couldn't stay on the seat. Once they collided, all three of them would have to start firing.

"Hold on," Cameron warned them.

Jodi braced herself for the impact, and she didn't have to wait long. It was only a couple of seconds before she jolted forward, and she heard the slam of metal crashing into metal. Someone yelled out in pain. Probably the gunman in the second car. But that didn't stop the shots. They continued to come at them, shredding what was left of the front and back and windshields.

"Cameron, get down," Gabriel warned him.

Gabriel took aim at whoever was continuing to shoot at them from the second car. That made him an easy target for whoever was behind them. Jodi unbuckled her seat belt, came up on her knees and pivoted in that direction.

And fired.

She took out the shooter who was on the passenger's side. That didn't stop the driver, though.

"He's about to hit us," Jodi shouted, but the words had barely left her mouth when the first car slammed into them.

The jolt sent her flying into both Gabriel and the back of the seat. Her shoulder was hit so hard that it nearly knocked the breath out of her. Gabriel didn't fare much better. He landed partially over the front seat with his head just a few inches from Cameron. That wasn't good. Because the other shooter in the first car was clearly trying to kill him.

Gabriel fixed that.

Cursing, he emptied his clip into the driver of the second car.

The shots stopped then.

From that direction anyway. They continued behind them, and while Gabriel reloaded, both Cameron and she returned fire. She wasn't sure which of them managed to hit the driver, but she finally saw him slump forward onto the steering wheel.

Not dead, though.

He was groaning in pain.

Gabriel finished reloading and threw open the cruiser door. "Cover me," he said, the urgency not just in his voice but in his movements, as well. "I need to get to him before he dies."

GABRIEL CURSED HIMSELF for being too late. He couldn't go back and undo the attack, but in hindsight he should have never agreed to take Jodi to the jail. At least not without more backup. Now, they had four dead men on their hands, and he still didn't have any answers. Because the fourth one had died before Gabriel could question him.

"Anything?" Jodi asked when his phone dinged with a text.

He glanced at the text from Jameson and shook his head. "No ID on the gunmen, but they're running the prints now. Jameson is rescheduling our visit to see your father. We'll go in the morning."

With plenty of extra security. No way did Gabriel want a repeat of today. Judging from Jodi's shell-shocked expression, neither did she.

She was no longer pacing. Probably because the spent adrenaline had left her too tired to do much of anything. Still, she was searching through Sentry's archived files, trying to find anything that could help them with their investigation. She almost certainly didn't feel like doing that, but it was better than focusing on the fact that they'd come damn close to dying again.

"I nearly got Cameron and you killed," she said, glancing up at him. "I'm sorry."

So that was the reason for the look on her face. Not because she'd been in danger but because Cameron and he had been. Both of them were fine, literally not a scratch on them, but Jodi wasn't seeing that, only the possibility that it could have been much, much worse.

Gabriel sighed and sank down on the sofa beside her. His own legs were feeling the effects of the adrenaline, too, but he was afraid if he stopped moving, he'd crash. Still, he wanted to make something crystal clear, and it was best if he looked her straight in the eyes when he said it.

"Those men could have been after me," he reminded her. "We don't know why we're being attacked, but when the dust settles, I could be the one who owes you an apology."

She shook her head. "I'm the one who made myself bait, and in doing so, I put targets on all of us."

That theory only worked if their attacker was someone trying to cover up nearly killing Jodi ten years ago. But this might not have anything to do with that.

"Maybe your dad can give us some answers tomorrow," Gabriel added. Then, he paused. "Will it do me any good to ask you to stay at the sheriff's office while I go to the jail?"

"No," she immediately answered. "I'm going. Plus, if my father does know anything, he's far more likely to tell me than you. He still considers you the enemy."

No way could he argue with that. Because Gabriel considered Travis the enemy, as well.

"If anyone stays behind, it should be you," Jodi went on. "I can't imagine it'll be easy for you to see the man convicted of murdering your parents."

"It won't be. But I'd visit Travis a thousand times if it meant stopping another attack. Besides, it'll be just as hard for you since he was also convicted of attempting to kill you."

She made a sound of agreement and took a deep breath. "Being here brings it all back." Another deep breath. "But it's not all bad. I'd forgotten that."

Yeah. Easy to forget the good stuff after being knifed and left for dead on the very land where she'd played as a child.

"For as long as I can remember, I've had a crush on you," she said. She winced a little, probably because she hadn't meant to say that out loud.

"I know," he admitted, since she had been so honest. "You used to follow me around and talk to Ivy about me. Once you turned eighteen, she started trying to play matchmaker."

Jodi nodded. "But she didn't get to play it for long. Ivy and I left for college, and when I came back, you were dating that lawyer from over in Appaloosa Pass. When I finally caught you in between women, it was too late."

Because the attack had happened.

The timing had certainly sucked.

"I'm the one who found you," Gabriel admitted. "You didn't remember?"

"No." She stayed quiet a moment and repeated it.

Hell. He shouldn't have brought that up because she got that haunted look again, the one that was deep in her eyes.

"You did CPR on me," she whispered.

Gabriel wanted to drop this, but Jodi was staring at him, waiting for him to say something. "Do you remember that or did someone tell you?"

She moved the laptop to the table, motioned toward her head. "I get little flashes of memories. Pieces. Most of them I push away because of, well, just because. But I remember a little of the CPR. You saved my life."

Believing that had helped him get through some god-awful nightmares, but Gabriel wasn't sure it was true.

She smiled a little. "I thought you were kissing me, but you were giving me mouth-to-mouth. You were giving me your breath."

He was, all the while cursing himself and praying that the ambulance would get there in time. Now, Gabriel cursed himself again because he leaned in and kissed her. Much, much better than mouth-to-mouth and the memories of that.

Well, better for him anyway.

But as he'd done in his office, he pulled away to make sure Jodi was okay with this. Apparently, she was because she slipped her hand around the back of his neck and drew him to her.

No.

That was the thought that went through his mind. Jodi's hand slide was the same as a green light. One that could lead straight to sex. And that couldn't happen. This went back to the bad-timing thing again, but he certainly didn't push her away when she kissed him.

It was Jodi who deepened the kiss. Jodi who pulled him so close to her that they were touching in plenty of the wrong places. Or the right places, he amended, if they were going to have sex.

But they weren't.

She moved, angling herself so that her leg was on the outside of his thigh. Not fully in his lap but close. The kiss, which was already too hot, turned even hotter, and the heat slid right through him. Hard to think with that kind of fire going on inside him. And his body reacted all right.

He went rock hard.

Unlike Jodi. She seemed to be softening. Her silky skin, against his. Her moving in for the taking. Gabriel had to do something to stop this or at least cool it down to give her time to think. Because once she thought about it, Jodi would probably decide this just wasn't a good idea.

"You're a virgin, aren't you?" he said when she

broke for air. She also stopped her hand, which was in the process of going to his stomach.

She didn't have to confirm it because he saw in her expression that the answer was yes. Of course, she was. This was a woman who had panic attacks when a man touched her. Well, most men anyway. She didn't seem to be having trouble with the touching now.

She studied his eyes as if trying to figure out what was going on in his head, and she cursed. "I missed my window of opportunity for sex. Because I wanted you to be my first. And then…afterward, because I didn't want to be with anyone."

He got that. "But if we have sex now, it's going to complicate things." That was not only stating the obvious but putting it mildly.

She nodded. "Plus, there's that whole commitment thing you don't want. But what if we take commitment off the table? What if this is only about sex for us?"

Gabriel gave her a flat look to let her know that wasn't possible. She must have believed it, too, because Jodi cursed again and moved off him.

"It would have been a bad idea anyway," she said, but it didn't sound as if she believed it.

Because he still had an erection, Gabriel didn't believe it, either.

Thankfully, his phone buzzed again, giving them a

much-needed interruption, and since it was Jameson's name on the screen, it could turn out to be important.

"It didn't take long for us to get IDs on the dead guys," Jameson said the moment Gabriel answered. He put the call on speaker so Jodi could hear. "That's because all four had prints in the system. Kevin McKee, Scott Hartman, Walter Bronson and Barry Hiller."

She repeated the names and shook her head. "I don't recognize any of them."

"Neither do I," Gabriel agreed. "What do you know about them?"

"That they're not from here. McKee and Hiller are from Houston. The other two are from Laredo. There's something not quite right about this," Jameson added. "These guys were thugs. Long police records. Drug users. In and out of jail. Not the sort to hire out for an attack on two lawmen and a security specialist."

Gabriel thought about that for a moment. "You believe they were hired because they'd work cheap?"

"That's exactly what I'm thinking. I'm betting these clowns came after you for just a couple of thousand dollars."

Which would make it next to impossible to find a money trail. Any of their three suspects could have that kind of cash on hand. Still, it had to be a risk to hire someone who was underqualified and maybe even high.

And Gabriel thought that might point to Hector. Because Jodi's boss dealt with criminals like this.

"Did these thugs have cell phones?" Gabriel asked.

"No. No IDs on them, either. Nothing in their pockets and nothing in the cars. We might be able to get something on those, but they're late models, so it's possible the person behind this bought them used through someone online."

Again, hard to trace that.

"I'll keep looking," Jameson said. "We can't keep having this string of bad luck."

You'd think they would get a break. Gabriel just hoped it was sooner than later.

He was about to thank his brother, but Jameson spoke before Gabriel could say anything. "Hold on a second. I'm getting another call from Cameron."

Cameron was supposed to be home, having some downtime after the attack, but Gabriel suspected the deputy was already back at work. He certainly would be, but he didn't want to have to take Jodi out in the open. They'd already had one attack too many today.

The seconds crawled by with Jodi making uneasy glances at him and the phone. It seemed to take an eternity for Jameson to come back on the line, and when he did Gabriel knew it was bad because Jameson cursed.

"It's Billy," Jameson said. "Someone murdered him."

Chapter Twelve

Every muscle in Jodi's body seemed to be aching, and her head was throbbing. That probably had a lot to do with the fact that she hadn't slept and was using caffeine to help her stay alert.

It wasn't a good idea to go into a visit with her father when she couldn't think straight, but she had no choice. Now more than ever, they needed answers.

Because someone had murdered Billy.

The one person who could have possibly cleared all of this up.

It was hard to grieve for him. After all, Billy had likely murdered a cop, but he'd no doubt been manipulated into it. It was a sick, dangerous person who would do something like that to a mentally disturbed teenager.

A smart person, too.

According to the preliminary report, someone had injected Billy with a lethal dose of barbiturates. And the suspect? His high-priced lawyer, Mara Rayburn. The problem, though, was that Mara was missing.

"Are you okay?" Gabriel asked, pulling Jodi out of her thoughts. He was seated next to her in the prison visiting area where they were expecting her father to arrive at any minute. He wouldn't actually be in the room with them but rather on the other side of some thick Plexiglas.

"I'm okay about this visit," she said, choosing her words. The rest of her was pretty much spent. She was tired and confused. Confused not just about who wanted to kill them but also her feelings for Gabriel.

Until she'd come back to Blue River, Jodi had been so certain that what she'd once felt for him was long gone. She had also been sure that she would never again want a man to touch her.

Well, she'd been wrong about that.

She had certainly wanted Gabriel to touch her after the latest attack. Even after "sleeping" on it, she should have realized that would be a mistake. But it didn't feel as if it'd be one. And that was a problem. Because the last thing they needed right now was to have their thoughts straying in the wrong direction. She had a strong suspicion that handing Gabriel her virginity would drop them smack-dab in the "wrong direction" category.

"It'd be so much easier if I hated you," she admitted. That caused him to smile. Which, in turn, caused her to go all warm.

She so didn't have time for this.

"Part of you probably does hate me," he answered.

He was talking about the attack now, but somehow even it had changed in her mind. Not the attack itself but rather her blaming Gabriel. He'd saved her, and no part of her body or mind was going to let her forget that.

The side door finally opened, and Jodi felt herself go stiff when she spotted her father. The past eight years had obviously been hard on him, and he looked several decades older than he actually was. But his eyes seemed to be clearer than ever. Probably because he wasn't drinking.

Her father glanced at Gabriel, and she didn't see a trace of the bitterness that she'd expected. In fact, Travis nodded a friendly greeting to him, then to her as the guard ushered him to the chair behind the glass. He didn't move fast because both his hands and feet were chained, and those chains rattled as he sank down across from them.

"Thank you for coming," he said. His voice had aged, too. It cracked from the hoarseness. "It's good to see you, finally." He stopped, and it seemed as if he was trying to rein in his emotions. "God, I've missed you."

"I miss you, too. And it's good to see you, but it's not a social visit," Jodi clarified.

She hated that she had practically snapped it because it put some sadness in her father's eyes. Since he was a convicted killer, he didn't need anyone, especially her, to add sadness to the obvious miserable life he already had behind bars.

Travis nodded. "I suspected as much. Still, I'm glad you're here. I think about you all the time."

Jodi could say the same about him. In fact, she gave him too much thought, considering that remembering him only brought back the images of the night she'd nearly died.

Well, mostly that's what it brought back.

There were other memories of those times when he hadn't been so drunk that he had been a father to her. That didn't make this visit easier. Because part of her—the girl who hadn't been stabbed yet—wanted to hang on to those rare good times, and she couldn't. She didn't want that coming into play as she tried to get to the truth.

Travis shifted his attention to Gabriel. "This is about the attacks?"

"Yeah. How did you know about them?" Gabriel asked.

"August." A weary sigh left his mouth. Maybe his brother was wearing on his nerves the way he was wearing on everyone else's. "He visits me at least once a week. He thinks all this mess that's going on will help clear my name, but the only thing I want is for them to stop." He paused. "Were either of you hurt?"

Jodi shook her head. "But some gunmen were

killed. Thugs. So was a teenage boy who got caught in the middle of this. Did August happen to mention that? Better yet, did he say anything about hiring them?"

Her father didn't seem surprised by the questions, and he certainly didn't jump to defend his brother. However, his mouth did tighten, the way it would when a person was going to have to talk about something unsettling.

"I told August that he'd better not do a single thing to harm you. Or you," he added to Gabriel. "You've both been through enough hell."

Yes, they had, but Jodi suspected the trip through Hades was far from being over. Until they had a name, the attacks would continue and wouldn't stop until someone else was dead.

"Did August say anything to implicate himself in these attacks?" Gabriel asked.

"No. He's too smart for that. Too loyal to me, as well." Travis groaned, shook his head. "God knows I don't deserve it."

Her father had definitely changed. This wasn't the defiant drunk who'd made so many people's lives miserable. Including hers. He'd never been physically abusive, but he'd had a razor-sharp tongue and an awful temper when the booze was in him. And the booze was often in him.

"I'm sorry," her father continued, still talking to Gabriel. "I'm scared for Jodi and you. Equally scared

for your brother and sisters. For Theo. But I honestly don't know who's behind what's going on. If
it's August, he hasn't given me any hint of it. And he
won't. First, because he knows I absolutely wouldn't
approve. Plus, he also knows our conversations are
being recorded."

"What about Russell?" she asked. "He visited you.
Did he mention anything about what's been going
on?"

Travis nodded. "He did, but he didn't bring up the
attacks. It's the second time he's come. He was here
a few years back, not long after I was convicted."

This was the first she was hearing of that original
visit. But then she hadn't exactly stayed in touch with
either Russell or her father. Still, she had to wonder why Russell would have done that. It wasn't as
if Russell and she had ever had a real relationship.

"What did Russell want?" Gabriel pressed.

"The first time he came, it was because he was
mad about being a suspect in the murders and in
Jodi's attack. He said it'd messed up his life, and he
blamed me. Russell thought if I'd just confessed right
off, that he wouldn't have been brought into it. But
I couldn't confess to something I didn't remember."

Since Gabriel's arm was touching hers, she felt
him tense. Probably because this was bringing back
the mother lode of memories for him.

"I still don't remember," Travis added, "but I'm
not whining about being innocent. Because I'm prob-

ably not. There was enough evidence to convict me, and I'll live with that. Die with it, too," he said under his breath.

She wasn't immune to hearing him spell everything out so clearly. No matter what he'd done, he was still her father, and she felt that biological connection tug at her. It was probably doing a lot more than just tugging at Gabriel, though. It was likely twisting him inside, and that's why she slid her hand over his.

Gabriel glanced at her, their gazes connecting for just a second. Since his mouth tensed, he was probably questioning what she was doing, but it didn't take long before he gripped her hand in his.

"Russell said you two were back together," Travis commented.

That caused both Jodi and Gabriel to snap toward him. "We're not," she assured him. "In fact, Gabriel and I have never been together."

Best not to mention that kiss and near-sex from the night before. Especially since there was something much more pressing to ask.

Jodi looked straight in her father's eyes. "Why did Russell come to visit you this second time?"

"He said it was because of an email threat he got. He thought maybe I was behind it, and he was worried about his wife and baby. Can't say I blame him, especially considering somebody murdered that cop and keeps trying to murder you."

Those emails definitely hadn't been empty threats, so Travis was right about Russell's concern. Two people were dead, along with some gunmen, and Gabriel, Cameron and she had come close to dying. No way did Jodi want an innocent baby to be caught up in another round of gunfire.

"I told Russell I had no idea who was doing all of this," her father went on. "I mean, I get *fan* letters, if you can call 'em that, but I don't answer them. Those people who write those letters are sick. And none of them have ever said anything about copycatting the crimes to set me free. The guards can verify that because they read everything before it comes to me." He paused again. "But I got the feeling Russell was here for more than just concerns about that email."

"What do you mean?" Gabriel snapped, taking the question right out of Jodi's mouth.

"Russell asked if I remember seeing anything that night. Specifically, he wanted to know if I remembered seeing Hector March around the Beckett ranch before or after the murders. I didn't know Hector, so Russell showed me a picture of him."

Maybe Russell was doing what Gabriel and she were—following the leads. But that wasn't a safe thing to be doing if he truly wanted to keep his wife and baby out of this. If Gabriel and she had found out Russell had visited the prison, then Hector or August could have learned it, too.

"And had you seen Hector?" Jodi pressed when her father didn't continue.

"He sort of looked familiar, but I couldn't be sure. Remember, I was drinking a lot in those days, and it's hard to sort it all out in my mind. It's possible, though, that I saw him at my trial."

Gabriel looked at her, no doubt wondering if that could have happened, and she had to nod. Hector had indeed come to the courthouse on the day she'd had to testify. He hadn't come into the courtroom itself, but he'd been in the hall, so there was a chance that her father had gotten a glimpse of him.

"August said you might be remembering more of what happened to you ten years ago," Travis said.

This was tricky territory. If she told the truth and admitted there were no new memories, it wouldn't stop the danger because her attacker might think she was lying. Besides, she wasn't sure she wanted to share any info like that with her father because he might just pass it along to August.

Plus, she *was* remembering.

When Gabriel had kissed her, her mind had slipped into a dreamy haze. Maybe it was because the kiss had caused her to relax, and she'd gotten some bit of the memories of him trying to revive her on that blood-spattered trail. If that had come back, maybe some of the other pieces would, too.

"I recalled the sound of his footsteps," she said. It was the truth. But that was a memory she'd had right from the start. "And grabbing the knife." That was a lie, but the prints proved she'd touched it.

"But you don't remember seeing his face?" her father pressed.

She studied his eyes, looking for any sign that he was worried about her recovering that particular memory, and she did see some concern. However, she didn't think it was for him but, rather, for her.

Jodi shook her head. "What about you? Have you remembered anything? Maybe dropping the knife? If you had done that, then someone else could have picked it up and used it on me."

Now, it was her father's turn to shake his head. "There are gaps in what went on that night, and some of that is just blank space. I remember arguing with Gabriel's dad about our cows that were breaking through his fences. After that, I got drunk, and I recall seeing Cameron. He took my truck keys 'cause I was trying to drive off from the bar, and he had somebody take me home. I kept drinking when I got there."

And she hadn't been at the house to stop him because she'd been at the Becketts. Of course, Cameron blamed himself, too, since he hadn't just arrested Travis and locked him up for the night. Jodi had given up on wondering "what might have been," but it was as if the fates had worked to bring about the murders and her attack.

"Other than the memories of drinking once I got

home," her father went on, "there's nothing after that until the deputies found me by the river. I don't have a clue how I got there."

It was the same story her father had told after he'd been taken into custody, and it hadn't changed a bit over the years. She didn't know if that meant it was the truth or if he had made sure there were no variations to prove he was lying. Too bad she might never know which it was.

"Tell me about Hattie Osmond," Gabriel said, surprising her. Surprising her father, too, judging by the way his forehead bunched up. "Did you ever see her with August?"

"Probably. I mean, she lived not far from us. Why?"

Gabriel lifted his shoulder. "It might be nothing, but it's possible someone was milking money from her."

Travis stayed quiet a moment. "And you believe it could have been August?" He didn't wait for Gabriel to confirm that. "If it was him, then that would give him motive for murdering your father?"

Bingo. But she could tell from her dad's expression that it was a connection he wasn't going to make. Or else he didn't want to make.

Travis dragged in a weary breath. "August has been good to me, and I talk to him a lot. Never once has he hinted that I'm here because of something he did."

That didn't mean it wasn't true. And it could explain why August was so hell-bent on clearing her father's name. What was missing, though, was any kind of proof. However, if they could connect August to the recent attacks, they might be able to get him to confess to things that happened a decade ago.

"Visiting time's up," one of the guards said to them. Both guards then went to Travis and helped him stand.

Travis made eye contact with her. "Thanks for coming." Then, he shifted his attention to Gabriel. "Don't let this SOB get to her again."

Gabriel nodded, but Jodi knew this was out of Gabriel's hands. He had already tied up three of his deputies just so they could make this trip to the prison. But he couldn't keep that kind of protection detail on her forever. That meant she either had to go into hiding or bring this monster out into the open.

She preferred doing the latter.

She'd lived enough of her life in the shadows, fearing another attack. Maybe it was time to face this head-on and, one way or another, bring it to an end.

Gabriel and she walked out after they ushered her father away. The moment they were back in the entry, Gabriel got back his weapon and phone, and he immediately called Cameron. Probably so the deputy could bring the cruiser to the front of the building.

"There's a problem," she heard Cameron say from the other end of the line.

Gabriel cursed and moved her to the side away from the door. "What happened?" he snapped.

"We found Billy's lawyer. And it's not good news."

Chapter Thirteen

Dead.

Gabriel wondered just how high this body count was going to go before he could finally arrest someone and put a stop to it. The latest casualty was Mara Rayburn, Billy's high-priced attorney, but in the end she hadn't fared any better than her client. Because now both of them had been murdered.

The moment Gabriel had Jodi in the back seat of the police cruiser, Cameron handed him his phone so that Gabriel could see what the SAPD officer had sent him about Mara. While Gabriel did that, Cameron started driving away from the prison. Fast. He was following Gabriel's orders since he didn't want Jodi on the roads any longer than necessary.

There was another cruiser directly behind them with two deputies inside. Jace Morrelli and Edwin Clary. All of them were prepared for a possible attack, but Gabriel hadn't braced himself nearly enough for the picture that was on Cameron's phone. One obviously taken from the most recent crime scene at the lawyer's condo.

The woman had been stabbed multiple times and had died in a pool of her own blood.

Jodi cursed, glanced away from the phone, and Gabriel cursed himself for not screening her from seeing the images. She already had enough nightmares without adding this.

"While you were inside talking to Travis, I've been getting a lot of updates," Cameron went on after he mumbled an apology to Jodi. An apology that she waved off, and she probably would have gone back for a second look at Mara if Gabriel hadn't handed Cameron the phone. "The ME doesn't have an exact time of death yet, but it appears she died shortly after Billy was killed."

So, if they went with their theory that Mara had murdered Billy, then someone had probably done this to make sure she stayed silent. That someone was no doubt the person behind the attacks.

"Mara's coworkers believe she was having an affair," Cameron went on, "and they said she seemed upset lately, like maybe the affair wasn't going so well. Of course, she could have been upset because she was plotting to murder her teenage client. That means if we can find her alleged lover, then perhaps we find the person who really did this."

"Her coworkers didn't know who her lover is… was?" Jodi corrected.

"No. They said she kept it secret. Who knows if that was her choice, or her lover's."

Yes, because if the killer's plan all along was to manipulate Billy and then have Mara off him, then no way would this snake want people to know who he was. It might not have started out that way, though. The affair could have started first, and then both Mara and, therefore, Billy could have been roped into committing murder. Then again, Mara could have agreed to all of this to please the man she "loved," and when the man was through with her, he killed her.

"There's more," Cameron continued. "Mara had a connection to our four dead thugs."

"I'm listening," Gabriel assured him. And so was Jodi. She'd moved to the edge of her seat.

"She once defended one of them, Walter Bronson, when she was doing pro bono work, and her coworkers said he recently showed up at her office. The thugs were friends, so it's possible she only had to convince Bronson to go after us yesterday, and he brought his buddies along to help."

That made sense, but Gabriel was betting that Mara hadn't been pleased about the gunman going to her office. "Is there a money trail that leads to Mara?" Gabriel asked.

"She withdrew about three grand yesterday morning. That could have been a partial payment or payment in full. I'm guessing the thugs worked cheap."

Jodi made a soft groan. "They were willing to kill us for what was probably pocket change to Mara."

Gabriel heard the disgust in her voice. The pain, too. All of this had to be clawing away at her, and there was nothing he could do to stop it.

Not yet anyway.

"SAPD thinks Mara knew her killer," Cameron explained. "There were no signs of forced entry into her condo, no signs of a struggle. Her attacker had simply gone in and started stabbing her. Her phone was in her pocket, and she hadn't even taken it out."

As she'd done to him, Gabriel slipped his hand over Jodi's. Yeah, definitely clawing away at her.

"The CSIs are still going through her condo," Cameron said a moment later. He, too, was checking Jodi's response in the rearview mirror. "Maybe they'll find something there to connect her to this secret lover. I told them to specifically look and see if there's anything to indicate if that lover could be Hector, Russell or August."

Jodi nodded. "That would be nice if it were all tied in a neat little package. But I doubt she left anything behind, and even if she had, the killer would have taken it." She paused. "What about surveillance cameras at her condo?"

"There weren't any, but SAPD said they'd check traffic cameras. If we have video proof that either Hector, August or Russell was near her condo, that might be enough to get an arrest warrant."

Coupled with the other circumstantial evidence they'd found, it should be, but they were still a long way from putting someone behind bars. Plus, SAPD would have jurisdiction in this, so Gabriel might not be able to interrogate a suspect even if the San Antonio cops did manage to take someone into custody.

"You want me to take you two back to the office or to your place?" Cameron asked.

One look at Jodi, and Gabriel knew the answer. She was exhausted and probably hungry. "To my house." Other than interviewing suspects, he could do pretty much everything else from his home office.

Jodi moved back, resting her head against the seat, and she closed her eyes. Gabriel doubted she was actually sleeping. More like trying to get rid of the images of seeing a butchered woman. No way for him to get rid of it. Because it had triggered the memories of how he'd found Jodi.

Since there was nothing he could say to her to help, Gabriel decided to get some work done. He texted Jameson to find out if he'd learned anything new on any of the legs of the investigation. No updates with the exception that his brother had managed to get access to Hector's bank account. Since Hector was a security expert, Gabriel doubted he'd left a money trail, but if someone had used such a trail to try to set the man up, then that part of it might be traceable.

The miles and minutes crawled by with Gabriel

checking his phone while he continued to keep watch around him. Cameron and the other deputies were no doubt doing the same, but there wasn't even a hint of trouble.

Not until Cameron arrived at the ranch. That's when Gabriel spotted someone he didn't want to see on the front porch of the old house, the one where his parents had been murdered.

August was waiting for them on the steps.

His car was parked on the side by some shrubs.

Jodi groaned, and that's when Gabriel realized her eyes were not only open but that she, too, had spotted her uncle. "What's he doing here?" she muttered.

Gabriel didn't know, but he intended to find out fast and then get rid of him. No way did he want one of their suspects hanging around Jodi or anywhere near the ranch.

Cameron pulled to a stop, and Gabriel threw open the door. "Wait in the cruiser," he told both of them. Cameron would, but he figured Jodi had no intention of doing that.

August stood, staggering a little, and that's when Gabriel noticed he had a bottle of whiskey on the steps where he'd been sitting. "You had Jameson haul me in like a common criminal," August snarled.

"Not common," Gabriel corrected. "You're a suspect in a murder investigation. That makes you far from common."

"Well, I didn't do it." His words were slurred, so

he was clearly past the "having a drink or two" stage. He certainly wasn't in any shape to drive, so that meant two deputies would have to take him home. Gabriel didn't like to split his security detail like that, but he hadn't planned on them staying once he had Jodi inside his house.

"I didn't have anything to do with those snakes," August went on, "or with trying to hurt Jodi. I wouldn't do that. Do you know how pissed off Travis would be with me if he thought for one minute that I'd tried to hurt his little girl?"

"He wouldn't be happy," Jodi said, stepping from the car. "Now, what do you want?"

"I want you to tell everyone that I'm not guilty of all this bad stuff I'm getting accused of. I'm just doing what you should be doing—busting your butt to clear your daddy's name so he won't end up dying behind bars."

"You sound like a man with a guilty conscience," Gabriel remarked. He moved away from August so he could stand near Jodi. He also motioned for Cameron and the other deputies to keep watch. He didn't want Jodi gunned down while trying to get info from a drunk man.

August shot him a glare. It didn't last because August staggered again and had to catch on to the step railing to stop himself from falling.

"Russell's wife came to see me this morning," August went on. "Tracy. She's a pretty little thing, but she was boo-hooing about her husband. She's scared he's going to be hurt or killed because of Jodi."

"Was Russell with her?" Gabriel asked.

"No. And she said I wasn't to tell him, that he wouldn't like it if she stuck her nose in his business."

Interesting choice of words, but of course, Gabriel was hearing it secondhand, so there was no telling what she'd actually said. Still, it wouldn't hurt for someone to question the woman. While he was at it, he could arrange for Hector's employees to be interviewed, as well.

"Take August home," Gabriel instructed Cameron.

August didn't put up an argument. He started for the cruiser just as Gabriel went with Jodi to the second one.

"I told Hector about you and Jodi," August said, stopping in his tracks. Jodi quit walking, too.

"Told him what?" she asked.

"That you two were sleeping together." August smiled, and it wasn't a pleasant one. "Want to know what Hector said?" he continued before Gabriel or Jodi could say anything. "He called you an ungrateful bitch and said you'd be sorry."

JODI HAD CERTAINLY been called worse than the *B*-word. But never by Hector.

"August could be lying," Gabriel reminded her.

He could be. In fact, he probably was. But there

was some truth in what he was saying. If Hector did indeed believe that Gabriel and she were lovers, then he wouldn't be happy about that. Jodi had seen how he'd behaved in the past couple of days, and plain and simple, he was jealous.

"I need to find a new job," she said as they made their way into Gabriel's house.

He immediately set the security system and moved her away from the windows. She was already heading away from them anyway since she wanted to sit down on the sofa. Her legs no longer felt steady.

"I could hire you as a deputy," Gabriel offered.

She looked at him and saw that he was already regretting that. "I doubt it would work out. Since you'd be my boss."

No need to say more, because it was clear that this attraction wasn't going away. Best not to bring that into the workplace. And if she worked for him, that would put them in constant contact each day. He wanted that contact but didn't especially want her to have a job where she could be required to put her life on the line.

Gabriel glanced out the window and gave a thumbs-up to Deputy Jace Morrelli, who'd be patrolling the grounds. There was a lot of ground to cover, which meant all of them were far from safe, but they couldn't keep everything fully guarded.

"Besides," she went on a moment later. "I have that badge-phobia thing." She was only half kidding, but the thought kept coming back to her—badges hadn't done a darn thing to keep his folks from dying or her from being attacked. "I need to find something that doesn't involve Hector."

Jodi cursed when her voice cracked. Cursed even more when the tears burned her eyes. "I'm not crying about Hector," she insisted. "I just hate knowing that I dragged you into this."

There was suddenly a lot of cursing going on, and it was coming from Gabriel. He sank down next to her. "Whatever you're thinking, the answer is no. You're not going to make yourself bait to protect me, and you're not going on the run to try to distance me from the danger."

Since those were the exact things she'd been thinking about doing, she just gave him a flat look. Well, as flat as she could manage, considering she was very close to tears again.

"I'm so tired of being afraid," she admitted. Of course, that wasn't the right thing to say to help with the tears or to steady her nerves. But Gabriel had something that worked.

He kissed her.

Even though he was already right there next to her, she hadn't seen the kiss coming, and despite the sizzle of heat she instantly felt, it didn't seem to be one generated by passion on his part. She figured that out when he pulled back, and she saw his eyes.

"You're distracting me," she said.

He certainly didn't deny it. "Did it work?"

It did. And there was no need for her to confirm that with words because the corner of his mouth kicked up. The smile didn't last, but he did brush his fingers on her cheek. Then, groaned.

"Eventually we're going to land in bed." His voice was a husky whisper. "I'm just trying for it not to be now. I don't think you could handle *now*."

Jodi wanted to assure him that she could, but that was attraction nudging her in his direction. The truth was, she could have a panic attack when they were only a few kisses in. She'd had attacks triggered by far less contact.

He didn't say anything for several moments, but she could see the debate he was having with himself. A debate he apparently lost.

Because he kissed her again.

This time she didn't feel the doubt or hesitation. And it didn't seem to be a distraction, either. Gabriel kissed her, sliding his hand around the back of her neck and pulling her to him.

Her stomach fluttered. Her heart began to race. It took her a moment to realize that it wasn't the beginnings of panic, but rather, it was pleasure.

Mercy, was it ever.

The heat from his kiss warmed her from head to toe, and she let that silky feeling wash over her. It both calmed and excited her, and it didn't take long before Jodi put her arms around him.

"You can stop this at any time," he assured her.

His voice only made her hotter. Of course, the kiss that followed his "stop" reminder probably had plenty to do with that increase in heat. The old feelings returned. Those days when she'd daydreamed about being with Gabriel just like this. Her, in his arms. Him, kissing her.

He lowered his hand from her neck to her back, all the while nudging her closer. Definitely no feelings of panic from this kind of contact. It felt natural.

Necessary.

As if she'd been starved for a very long time and was finally getting what she needed. And apparently what she needed was Gabriel.

He lowered the kisses to her neck, pausing between each one, no doubt to give her a chance to tell him to stop. But Jodi couldn't see herself saying that anytime soon.

She moved her hand, too. To his chest, and she slid her fingers over the muscles there. All toned and perfect, Gabriel had always had a great body. She got to see some of that body when she undid the buttons on his shirt. Then, she touched bare skin and got a nice reward when he grunted with pleasure.

So, she touched him again. While he took those wildfire kisses lower, to the tops of her breasts, she pushed open his shirt. He was still wearing a shoulder holster, so she couldn't get it all the way off, but she saw enough of him to kick up her pulse another notch.

"Remember, we don't have to keep doing this," he repeated. He slipped his hand under her shirt and did some touching of his own. Each stroke of his fingers created new fires and sent her soaring.

Jodi forgot how to breathe.

And didn't care if she ever remembered.

He didn't take off her top. Maybe because he knew it would bother her for him to see the scars, but Gabriel did lower his head, and he kissed them, one by one. But he didn't stop there. He kept kissing, going lower to the front of her jeans.

Oh, man.

That was what she wanted, and it didn't take much of that before Jodi was searching for his zipper. He stopped her by unzipping her first. The touches on her stomach were mild compared to what she felt when he slid his hand into her jeans. And then her panties. He pushed his fingers through the slick heat he found and nearly caused her to scream.

In a good way.

The pleasure soared, so intense that Jodi wasn't sure she could take it. But she did. And Gabriel clearly had plans to do more than touch.

"Should we stop?" he asked.

"No." She didn't have to think about that, either.

She wasn't sure if he was relieved, but he did start to shimmy her jeans off her. Jodi helped, though she was trembling now. Not from fear or panic but because Gabriel kept adding some of those slick strokes in between the undressing.

By the time he had finally removed her jeans and panties, Jodi was more than ready to have him haul her off to bed. But he didn't do that. He hauled her onto his lap instead. She was about to protest, but then he kissed her again, and that rid her of any doubts that this was the right way to go.

She reached between them, finally locating his zipper, and she freed him from his boxers while he fumbled in his pocket. Then, his wallet. To take out a condom, she realized. Jodi had been so caught up in the heat of the moment that she'd forgotten all about safe sex. At least Gabriel had remembered.

There was just a jolt of panic when she saw him put on the condom, but again, that vanished when he kissed her. He also reminded her once again that they could stop. That's when Jodi took matters into her own hands. Literally. The moment Gabriel had gotten the condom on, she took hold of him and guided his erection inside her.

She got another jolt. Just a quick pinch of pain—that she ignored. Because there were much, much better feelings to focus on. Like this heat that was burning her from the inside out.

Gabriel didn't move. He gave her a moment, probably to adjust, but it wasn't a moment she wanted. Jodi started to move, and even though she didn't have a clue what she was doing, she went with what felt right.

He helped. Gabriel caught on to her hips with one hand, and he slid the other one between her legs. At first she had no idea why he'd done that. But she soon found out. He used those maddening touches in just the right place while the strokes inside her continued.

It didn't take long for her body to respond to that. In fact, it was too short. She wanted to hang on to this moment for a long, long time. But there was no way she could last. Gabriel made sure of that. He kept touching. Kept moving inside her. Until everything pinpointed to just him.

He pushed her right to the point where she could take no more. And then with one last touch, Gabriel sent her flying.

Chapter Fourteen

Gabriel hadn't remembered a mistake ever being this good. But despite the slack feeling he had from the great sex, he still had enough common sense to know that he shouldn't have done this.

This was a complication neither of them needed.

And it would be a complication all right. Not just because here he was holding her in bed but because he wanted to keep holding her.

He couldn't, and that's why Gabriel forced himself from the bed so he could pull on his jeans and go back into the living room to check his laptop. Even though it was already after regular duty hours, there could still be reports coming in. Updates. Hell, the world could have ended in the past couple of hours, and he wouldn't have even noticed it.

That's because he'd made another mistake by taking Jodi a second time.

She definitely hadn't said no, and he'd been counting on her doing just that. Because he certainly hadn't had the willpower to turn her away—as he'd done ten years ago.

He put on his shoulder holster—old habits—and grabbed a slice of leftover pizza from the fridge before he sat down to boot up his computer. Six emails from Jameson and all of them were about the dead lawyer. The first two weren't good news, either.

SAPD hadn't been able to find a security or traffic camera yet that had been at the right angle to see who'd gone into Mara's condo complex and knifed her to death. Jameson had managed a phone conversation with Russell's wife, Tracy, but it'd been a bust because Russell had told his wife to hang up—and she had. Russell might have just wanted to protect her, and he might not know that Tracy had paid August a visit.

Gabriel went to the next message. Photos of both Billy's and Mara's crime scenes. Photos that Jodi wouldn't be seeing. The next email was a lab report on the drugs Billy had been given, and which caused him to overdose.

And then Gabriel got to the last email.

Hell.

It was yet another picture, and according to Jameson, it was a note that the cops had found beneath Mara's body. It was just two words, scrawled on a piece of paper.

For Jodi.

If Gabriel had had any doubts that Billy's and

Mara's deaths weren't connected to what'd happened a decade ago, that would have cleared them up. Because it was linked even if it was solely due to someone trying to cover their tracks.

He heard Jodi stirring in the bedroom and immediately closed the email. A moment later, she came in. She yawned, pushed her hair from her face and smiled at him.

She'd gotten dressed, but she still looked rumpled. Damn attractive, too. The woman certainly knew how to make his body notice her. He also noticed her weapons. She had put them on, as well. Apparently, he wasn't the only one with some old habits. But despite the fact that they were behind locked doors and the security system was on, it still didn't feel safe.

Maybe no place would.

"Apparently, sex is the cure for panic attacks," she said. "Or maybe you're the cure. Either way, I'm hungry." She started toward the kitchen but then stopped. Probably because she'd noticed the worried expression on his face.

"What happened?" she asked.

It was a cheap, dirty trick, but he went to her and kissed her. He thought maybe she still had enough post-sex haze for it to work at distracting her. It didn't.

"Is someone else dead?" she pressed.

Since her mind was already leaping to a worst-case scenario, Gabriel knew he had to tell her the truth. Or rather, show her. He reopened the email and turned the laptop so she could see the message and Jameson's remark.

"Oh." That's all she said for several seconds, and then Jodi sat on the sofa. "I guess whoever's after me wants to rub salt in the wound."

It seemed that way to Gabriel, as well. And he was afraid the salt-rubbing would continue with another attack. That was probably why he went on full alert when he heard the movement in front of his house. Gabriel jumped to his feet, and in the same motion he drew his gun. Jodi drew her weapon as well, but he made sure he was in front of her when they went to the window to look out.

And he cursed.

"Hector," he said under his breath.

Jodi's boss was in the front yard. And he wasn't alone. Deputy Jace Morrelli was with him, and judging from Jace's expression, he wasn't any more pleased about this visit than Gabriel was. Not only was Hector a suspect, his car wasn't anywhere in sight, which meant he might have been trying to sneak up on them and that Jace had caught him.

Hector looked up at the window, making eye contact with Gabriel, and while the man didn't have a gun in his hand, Gabriel figured he was heavily armed. That's why Gabriel told Jodi to stay back. He disarmed the security system and opened the door just a fraction.

"What the hell are you doing here?" Gabriel demanded.

Hector spared him a glance. "Protecting Jodi. Something that I've been doing quite well for the past ten years. She comes back here, to you, and twice someone's tried to kill her."

"Because her attacker is afraid she's remembered his face. You think it's your face she'll remember?"

Now, Hector did more than glance at him. He turned, his hard stare drilling into Gabriel. Even though the sun was already setting, and there wasn't a lot of light, Gabriel had no trouble seeing the hatred in the man's eyes. Or the fact that Hector was armed to the hilt, along with wearing a bulletproof vest.

"I told him to leave," Jace said.

Good. Because it saved Gabriel from telling Hector that himself.

"I was just going back to my car," Hector insisted. "There's no law against a man sitting in his own car on the road." He made an uneasy glance around. "Someone's trying to set me up. Maybe August or Russell."

"They claim someone's trying to set them up, too," Jodi said. "And they believe you might be doing that."

She stepped to Gabriel's side. Well, as much of his side as she could manage since he was taking up most of the doorway, and he didn't intend to go out on the porch with Hector where the man could maybe try to gun him down.

Hector nodded, readily admitting that. "One of us is probably guilty, and it isn't me. That means someone is making himself look bad to get the lime-light off him."

That was Gabriel's theory, too.

Hector shifted his gaze back to Jodi, and while she was fully clothed, Gabriel figured the man knew what had gone on tonight. What Gabriel couldn't tell was if Hector's tight expression was because he was jealous or just concerned about Jodi. Either way, he couldn't take the chance that it was the jealousy.

"Leave," Gabriel warned Hector.

For a couple of long moments, Gabriel thought he was going to have to arrest the man, but Hector finally turned and started walking away.

"Follow him to his car," Gabriel told Jace, and Gabriel intended to stand there and watch. If Hector was guilty and desperate, he might decide to try to shoot the deputy.

"Any chance Hector would have brought some of his security guys with him?" Gabriel asked while he glanced around the grounds.

"No. Hector works alone." She paused. "But if he's truly innocent, he could have come here with the hopes of trying to draw out the killer. Of course, that would only work if the killer was watching us."

Gabriel had the sickening feeling that he was. And

no, he wasn't ruling out Hector. In fact, the man could have come here to set up cameras or listening devices, which meant Gabriel needed to get some backup out here.

While continuing to keep watch, he took out his phone to do that, but something flashed in the corner of his eye. It wasn't Jace or Hector because this came from the opposite direction.

From his parents' old house.

The electricity was off, but there was definitely a light in the window. Maybe either a candle or a flashlight.

"Someone's inside," Jodi said under her breath. "Could it be Jameson?"

"No. He wouldn't go there." They had had trouble over the years with thrill-seeking teens, but Gabriel figured with everything going on, this was much more serious.

"You see that?" Jace called out, tipping his head to the house.

"Yeah. Don't go there just yet." And Gabriel called the sheriff's office to round up every available deputy.

However, before he could even press the number, a shot cracked through the air.

THE SOUND OF the bullet had barely registered in Jodi's mind when she felt herself being shoved back. That was Gabriel's doing. He rammed his shoulder into her and sent her flying backward.

She caught on to him to keep from falling, but Jodi also did that to pull him back, too. He immediately shut the door but then went straight to the window. No doubt to check on Jace.

Jodi hurried to the side window in the living room, which would give her the best view of his parents' house. She didn't stand directly in front of the glass, though, since it would make her an easy target. She stayed to the side so she would not only have a view of the old house but also that stretch of the road. What she didn't have a good view of, however, was the trail in between the two houses. Too many shrubs and trees.

Too many places for someone to hide.

Just as they'd done the night she was attacked.

She tried not to think of that now because it wouldn't help. The only thing she could do was keep watch to make sure someone didn't get close enough to fire another shot.

The light was still on upstairs in the old house, and it was flickering. Maybe because someone was moving it, but if it was a candle, it was possible the wind was blowing it since the window seemed to be open a couple of inches. It definitely hadn't been open when she'd visited the place two days ago.

From the other side of the room, she heard Gabriel call the sheriff's office and ask for backup. It wouldn't take the deputies long to get out here, but she prayed they wouldn't be driving into the middle of a gunfight.

But there were no other shots.

In fact, there were no other sounds, period. The place had suddenly gotten so quiet that the only thing she could hear was her own heartbeat drumming in her ears. And she wasn't sure that silence was a good thing. At least if she could have heard footsteps or spotted movement of some kind, she would have known where the shooter was.

"Is Jace okay?" she asked Gabriel.

"Can't tell, but he doesn't appear to have been hit. Hector and he are behind some trees."

Not ideal, because if Hector was the one responsible for the attacks, he could kill Jace. The deputy had to know that, of course, so maybe he was watching carefully to make sure that didn't happen.

"The shot couldn't have come from anywhere near my parents' house," she heard Gabriel say.

No, the angle was all wrong. Whoever had fired that shot was closer to where Hector's car was parked. Did that mean there were two attackers out there—one in the house and the other on the road?

Jodi glanced back at Gabriel, but he had his attention pinned to his side of the house. "Do you see anyone?"

"No. Maybe the person ran off after he fired." But Gabriel didn't sound very hopeful about that.

Part of Jodi didn't want this snake to run. She

wanted to go ahead and have a showdown, one that would put an end to the danger once and for all, but with Jace out there, and the other deputies on their way, that wasn't a good idea. There had already been too many murders, and she didn't want anyone else dying tonight.

A sound shot through the room, causing her to gasp, but it was only Gabriel's phone. Without taking his attention off their surroundings, he hit the answer button and put the call on speaker.

"Sorry that I didn't see the guy before he took a shot at us," she heard Jace say from the other end of the line.

"I didn't see him, either," Gabriel answered. "He must have come on foot from up the road."

"Yeah, that's what I figured, too. But I did get a glimpse of him. Male, wearing a ski mask like the other guys who attacked us. He ran into the woods across from your folks' house. That was just a couple of seconds after Hector and me got behind these trees, and I haven't seen the guy since."

So, maybe he had run after getting off that single shot, but the knot in her stomach told her that there was another reason he wasn't firing. Like because maybe he was getting in a better position to do more damage. This way, too, Gabriel was separated from his deputy, so not only didn't he have immediate police backup in the house, Jace was out there without backup, as well.

"I'm going after him," someone said. Hector. She had no trouble hearing him, either. "I'm not just going to cower here while he picks us off one by one."

"You're staying put," Gabriel told him.

But neither Jace nor Hector answered. Jace did curse, though, and there seemed to be some kind of scuffle going on. Mercy, no. Hector couldn't be doing this.

However, he was.

"The SOB punched me," Jace said, "and then he started running. You want me to go after him?"

Before Gabriel could answer, there was another shot, then another. Both came from the same area where the first one had been fired.

"Stay put and take cover," Gabriel told Jace. There was a franticness in his voice. In his movements, too, because he threw open the door, took aim and fired.

Jodi couldn't see the person Gabriel had shot at, and she didn't want to leave the window in case someone came in or out of the old house.

"Get back!" she shouted to Gabriel when a bullet smacked into the door frame right where he was standing.

He did get back, but cursing, he hurried to the front window and threw it open. Like her, he stayed to the side, and he fired out through the screen.

"I think I might have hit him," Gabriel relayed to her.

Good. She hoped he'd killed him because this was

probably a hired thug. Yes, they could possibly get answers from him, but the only way for that to happen was to get to him and arrest him. No way did she want Gabriel going out there.

"When Jameson gets here, I'll have him stay with you," Gabriel added. "Jace and I can go after this clown who shot at us. Hector, too."

Jodi shook her head. "The attacker will come to us, and when he gets close enough, we can kill him."

"Hector was right. This guy will try to pick us off, and he can sit out there and shoot at us until he gets us. We need to stop him."

She couldn't argue with that, but she didn't want Gabriel out there. He glanced at her, their eyes connecting, and even though he didn't say anything, the glance was a reminder that catching bad guys was his job. No way would he want to stay inside where it was safe while his deputies and heaven knew who else was in danger. But "safe" was where she wanted him to be.

This was about the sex.

It had indeed changed everything. And while even before tonight Jodi certainly hadn't wanted Gabriel hurt, now it cut her to the core to think of him being shot. Or worse.

Two more shots came at them, both of them smacking into the side of Gabriel's house. She doubted the bullets would be able to get through the walls, so maybe the gunman was doing this as a way of pinning them down.

But why?

She didn't like any of the answers that came to mind, but it was possible the shots were a distraction, meant to keep them occupied while someone sneaked closer to them. Jodi had already been keeping a close watch around them, but she tried even harder to pick through the near darkness and see someone.

And she did.

"Gabriel," she managed to say despite her breath having gone thin.

"Hell," Jace said only a few seconds later. Probably because the deputy had seen the same thing Jodi had.

Hector, coming out of the trees near the old house, and he wasn't alone.

The ski-masked thug was behind him and had a gun pointed right at Hector's head.

GABRIEL FELT A punch of dread and adrenaline. This was not what he wanted to happen, especially not without plenty of backup in place.

His first thought was this could be a ruse, one concocted by Hector to draw them out into the open. After all, Hector was a trained security specialist. But Gabriel knew firsthand that sometimes all the training and experience wasn't enough to keep thugs from getting to you.

Jodi moved away from the window, coming toward him. "You're not going out there," she said to him.

He was about to tell her the same thing, but if Hector was innocent, Gabriel didn't just want to stand by and watch an innocent man get killed. Especially since it appeared that the ski-masked guy had disarmed Hector.

"Call Hector right now," Gabriel instructed. "I need to see what this thug wants." And he also wanted to hear Hector's voice, to try to figure out what was really going on here.

Jodi nodded, and while she took out her phone and made the call, she also returned to the window to keep watch. Good. He hated having her near the glass where she could be shot, but Gabriel needed someone to keep an eye on that side of the house since it was essentially a blind spot for him.

Gabriel opened the front door, and while he didn't go onto the porch, he angled himself in the doorway so he could better see Hector. And also get a look at the guy in the ski mask. No way did Gabriel have a clean shot, but he wanted to be ready just in case.

Since he was watching Hector so closely, he saw when the man glanced down at Hector's pocket. Probably because his phone was ringing with the call from Jodi. His captor must have told him to answer it because a couple of seconds later, Hector reached in his pocket. Using just two fingers, he took out his phone, pressing the button on it and then lifting it in the air.

"Jodi," Hector answered. She put the call on speaker, so Gabriel had no trouble hearing the man.

Or the guy who had Hector at gunpoint.

"Do you want him dead?" the thug asked.

That was still to be determined, but for the moment Gabriel wanted both of these guys alive.

"I don't want Jodi coming out here," Hector said before Gabriel or she could answer.

"Neither do I," Gabriel assured him. "And it's not going to happen. She's staying inside, where she's safe." Hopefully.

"Then you're going to have to watch a man die," the gunman said.

Maybe it was a bluff, but every one of his lawman's instincts were yelling for him to stop this. If for no other reason than he didn't want Jodi to have to witness her boss and mentor being murdered in front of her.

"I might have a shot," Jodi mouthed, and she hit the mute button on her phone after she laid it on the window ledge. By doing that, she freed up both her hands. Probably to take that shot she'd just mentioned.

But Gabriel shook his head. "I don't want you that far out of cover. Besides, if you miss, you'll hit Hector."

Her mouth went flat, and she looked a little insulted that he'd even suggested she wouldn't be able to hit her intended target. "I'll aim for the goon's left leg. With the way he's standing, I can hit it, and when goes he down, Hector can get the gun away from him. Hector's probably already planning to elbow this guy in the gut or something."

Gabriel had figured that out. He just hoped it didn't get Hector killed. Because it was possible this guy wasn't alone. In fact, it was probable that he wasn't. Heaven knew how many *friends* he'd brought along with him. And if he wasn't holding his boss at fake gunpoint, then he could be out there, as well.

In the distance, Gabriel heard the sirens from the police cruisers, and that meant he had to make a decision now. He definitely didn't want his brother and deputies driving into a hostage situation.

"On the count of three, I'll fire over their heads," Gabriel finally told her. "You go ahead and try to hit the guy in the leg. If Hector moves out of the way, then one of us can take the kill shot."

She nodded, turned and didn't waste any time taking aim.

Gabriel wanted to count as fast as possible, so he could get her out of the line of fire. "One, two, three." And he pulled the trigger.

So did Jodi.

She didn't miss, either.

Her shot slammed into the thug's leg, and he howled in pain. The guy staggered back, and Hector went after him. If this was Hector's hired muscle, then Jodi's boss made the punch that he delivered look very convincing. Hector ripped the gun from the man's hand and took aim.

Just as another shot cracked through the air.

This one went right into Hector.

He fell, clutching his chest, but he didn't stay on the ground. Even though he was clearly struggling, Hector was trying to crawl toward the ditch.

"Oh, God." Jodi automatically turned as if ready to run out and help him.

"He's wearing a Kevlar vest," Gabriel reminded her.

But Kevlar wasn't going to help him if the wounded gunman shot him in the head. And that's what Gabriel thought he had in mind when the gunman whipped out another weapon from an ankle holster. When he took aim at Hector, Gabriel took aim at him.

And fired.

He went for the kill shot, two bullets to the head, since an injured hired gun could still do plenty of damage. The man fell back, his head smacking onto the ground. It gave Hector time to get into the ditch before the next shot came.

The second gunman was somewhere in the trees near the road. The very road where the cruiser would be arriving soon, so Gabriel fired off a quick text to let Jameson know to stay back until Jodi and he could figure a way to draw him out. Then, they could get an ambulance for Hector in case he was hurt.

"Watch out!" Gabriel heard Jace yell.

That's when Gabriel also heard something else. A car engine.

Gabriel pivoted, whipping around in Jace's direction, and saw a black car driving up the road. It was coming from the opposite direction of the cruiser, and the driver was speeding. He considered shooting into it, but it's possible this was someone who was merely in the wrong place at the wrong time.

It wasn't.

When the car reached the treed area where Jameson was, it veered off the road, and the driver, who was wearing a ski mask, jumped out. The car, however, continued to come right toward Gabriel.

"Run!" Gabriel shouted to Jodi. He hurried to her, caught on to her arm and got them moving toward the back of the house.

Not a second too soon.

The car rammed into the porch, and it wasn't just a simple crash. No.

The car exploded into a fireball.

Chapter Fifteen

Because of where she'd been standing, Jodi hadn't seen the car until she glanced back over her shoulder while Gabriel and she were running. It was an older model vehicle and obviously loaded with some kind of explosives for it to go up in flames like that.

Those flames could easily make it into the house.

Gabriel led her to the kitchen. No sign of any trouble here, but the smoke was already starting to make its way through the house. It reeked of gasoline, so maybe it hadn't actually been a real bomb. The person could have just filled the car with open containers of gas, and the impact could have triggered a spark.

"Who did this?" she asked, keeping her voice at a whisper.

What she wasn't able to do was tamp down all the fear and panic that was starting to roar through her. Gabriel's front porch was on fire. A fire that would no doubt spread—fast. And his brother, Jace and Hector were out there, maybe under attack right now. Since Gabriel and she could no longer see them, they couldn't help them. Not from the back of the house anyway.

"I don't know," Gabriel said, answering her question. He hooked his arm around her waist and moved her to the side of the fridge while he hurried to the back door to look out. "He was wearing a ski mask and jumped from the car."

Mercy. That meant the guy was still out there, and he had at least one hired gun to help him because there'd been the shot fired at Hector from the other end of the road. If Hector was innocent, she hoped he had managed to find some cover, because it was obvious things had gone from bad to worse.

"Keep watch behind us," Gabriel instructed. He opened the back door several inches.

Jodi did as he said, but she wouldn't be able to keep watch for long because of the smoke. It was getting thicker with every passing second, and soon they wouldn't be able to stay put. That meant going outside.

Where gunmen could be waiting for them.

What they needed was to get a better look at what was going on. Unfortunately, a better look came with risks. Because the moment they left the house, it could put them right in the line of fire.

"Call Jace," he said, passing her his phone. "Ask if he's got eyes on the driver of that car."

While she volleyed glances all around them, Jodi found his number and pressed it. She wasn't sure if the deputy would even be in a position to answer, but he did.

"Gabriel," Jace said. His voice was barely audible.

"It's me, Jodi. Are you okay?"

"For now." Jace whispered, as well. "The guy who was driving that car has to be nearby."

"Any idea where the other shooter or Hector is?" she asked.

"No. But you and Gabriel should get out of the house right now. The fire's spreading, and the fire department won't be able to get out here until we've rounded up these two thugs."

Jace was being optimistic that there were only two of them. There could be a dozen. She cursed the person who'd put all of this together.

"If Gabriel and you run out the back, I'll try to cover you," Jace said, ending the call.

There was no need for her to relay that to Gabriel since he'd been standing close enough to hear. He looked back at her, making eye contact, and he seemed to be saying he was sorry about all of this. Well, she was sorry, too, but only because she was probably the reason so many people were in danger right now.

Gabriel tipped his head to his truck that was parked out back. "That's where we're heading."

And he pressed the remote on his keys to unlock the doors.

He didn't remind her to keep watch or be careful because he knew that she would be. As careful as she could be anyway.

Gabriel used his shoulder to open the door wider, and he stepped out onto the porch. He took a quick look around before he motioned for them to get moving. She did. Gabriel barreled down the porch steps, and Jodi was right behind him. They made a beeline for the truck.

But didn't get far.

Jace fired, his bullets going well over their heads. But one shot slammed into his truck, right into the engine. Judging from the angle, this bullet had almost certainly come from the driver of the car that was up in flames. She doubted that a single shot had disabled it, but the gunman fired again.

And again.

These didn't go into the truck, though.

They came right at Gabriel and her.

They immediately dropped to the ground, both of them rolling to the side of the porch. It wasn't much protection, especially considering this new position possibly put them in the direct sight of Hector and the other gunman, but at least the driver's shots were no longer an immediate threat. Not to them anyway. The goon could turn that gun on Jace.

"We can't stay here," Gabriel said, but it sounded as if he were talking more to himself than to her.

But Jodi agreed. Eventually, the fire would make it back here, and the flames and smoke could kill them. Running to the truck was out, too, since it was obvious the shooter had a good angle on that.

"The barn," Gabriel added.

It was to the side of the truck, and while it would indeed provide some cover, they still had to get to it. There were some trees and shrubs dotting the way, but it was possible Gabriel and she could get caught in the cross fire.

Gabriel's phone dinged with a text message, and since she still had his cell, she read Jameson's text aloud. "Approaching on foot. Don't fire in our direction."

However, the words had no sooner left her mouth when someone did fire. Not the driver or Jace this time. The shot had come from the area where she'd last spotted Hector. Of course, that was the same general direction as Jameson and the other shooter, so it could be one of them. She prayed that Jameson was all right.

She put Gabriel's phone back in her pocket, so her hands would be free when they ran. Which she didn't have to wait long for. Almost immediately, Gabriel got them moving, but they didn't make it far before the shots came. Not a single bullet, either. But a hail of them. They had no choice but to get back on the ground behind one of the trees.

Jodi automatically maneuvered into a position that would allow her to keep watch behind them, and she hated that her pulse kicked up when she realized her area to watch was the very trail where she'd nearly died.

The sun had fully set now, but there was enough illumination coming from the fire that she could see it. At least she could see the trail itself. However, it was impossible to tell if anyone was hiding in those tall shrubs. The very ones her attacker had used ten years ago.

"See anything?" Gabriel whispered.

Before she could answer, the phone dinged, but this time, it wasn't Gabriel's. It was hers. Keeping watch, Jodi took it from her pocket. Not a text but rather a call, and it wasn't from Jace.

It was from Hector.

Gabriel mumbled some profanity under his breath when she showed him the name on the screen. Jodi pressed the answer button, but she didn't say anything. That's because this might not be Hector. The gunman could have finished him off, taken Hector's phone and could be using this call to pinpoint her location by listening for the sound of her voice.

"Jodi?" someone said from the other end of the line. She couldn't tell if it was Hector or not because the voice was a hoarse whisper. "Please," he said. "I need your help."

It was Hector all right.

"What's wrong?" she asked as softly as she could manage.

"I've been shot, and I'm bleeding out fast." Hector cursed. "I'm pinned down."

And then Jodi heard something she didn't want to hear. Another gunshot. Followed by Hector's sharp sound of pain.

GABRIEL HEARD THE sound that Hector made. And he got a glimpse of the stark expression on Jodi's face, too. She was no doubt torn between getting to her boss but balancing that with the real possibility that this could be a trap that could get her killed.

Especially since it would mean going on that trail between his and his parents' houses.

"I can't go out there," she whispered. Maybe to herself. Maybe to Hector.

She then hit the End Call button so she could text for an ambulance. One was almost certainly on the way. Jameson would have called for it, but the medics wouldn't come closer as long as there was gunfire.

And there was plenty of that.

Shots came from Jace's direction. From Hector's, too, and Gabriel couldn't tell who was doing the shooting. It was possible that Jameson was in on this by now, since he would have had a chance to at least reach the area where Hector was. Maybe his brother had managed to take out the gunman. Gabriel didn't have to remind Jameson to be mindful of Hector, too, since his brother already knew Hector was a suspect.

Perhaps a dead one, though.

"Should we try to make it to the barn or truck again?" she asked.

It was tempting—especially the truck since they could possibly use it to escape. But Gabriel shook his head, and he tried to pick through the sounds to make sure no one was sneaking up on them. He could hear…something, but it was hard to tell what it was exactly, thanks to the fire now snapping and eating through his house.

His *home*, he mentally corrected.

It twisted at his gut to see it being damaged like this, but there was nothing he could do to save it. Right now, his priority had to be keeping everyone alive.

"I'm sorry," someone called out.

Jace.

Gabriel pivoted in that direction and saw something he didn't want to see. Jace being held at gunpoint. It was almost identical to what had happened to Hector just minutes earlier with a ski-masked thug behind him. The guy had jammed a gun to Jace's head.

"I didn't see him before it was too late," Jace added.

Gabriel hated that Jace felt the need to apologize

for something like that, but it did put them in a really bad position. Because Gabriel figured he knew what was coming next, and he didn't have to wait long for it.

"Start running down the trail," the gunman said. "Or I'll shoot him where he stands."

Gabriel had obviously figured wrong. He'd expected the thug to tell Jodi and him to put down their guns. What kind of sick plan was this?

A bad answer immediately came to mind.

The same person who'd attacked Jodi ten years ago wanted a chance to finish her off in the same spot.

"And if we don't run?" Gabriel challenged.

The gunman fired a shot. Not into Jace's head. But rather his shoulder. At the same time, there was another shot—it came from Hector's direction—and Gabriel heard what was another loud groan of pain. Maybe Hector had been shot again. Maybe it was a ruse, but the ruse definitely didn't apply to Jace.

Jace dropped to his knees, the pain etched all over his face, and the gunman dropped with him, staying behind him so he could continue to use Jace as cover. Gabriel didn't have a clean shot, and he figured Jodi didn't, either.

"Run or I'll shoot him in his other shoulder," the gunman warned them. "The third shot will go in his gut. I'm thinking if you hadn't obeyed by the fourth shot, then your deputy will be a goner."

Hell, Jace might not survive the second, much less a third and fourth, shot. With the angle the clown was holding that gun, the bullet could go down Jace's shoulder and straight into his heart.

"Run!" the gunman shouted to them.

"We have no choice," Jodi said. Her voice was trembling a little, but that didn't stop her from turning in the direction of the trail.

Where someone was no doubt waiting to kill her.

"I can't let Jace die because of me," she added.

Gabriel couldn't let that happen, either, but he could take some precautions. "Stay low. I don't want this idiot gunning us down, and he might do that if we stand up. Crawl. And stay close to me."

Of course, that wouldn't stop anyone on that trail from shooting at them, too, but Gabriel figured the monster who was waiting there wanted to use a knife.

On Jodi.

Maybe that's why she pulled her own knife from her boot and clamped it between her teeth. The moment she did that, they started moving. Of course, there was no guarantee that the gunman holding Jace wouldn't just go ahead and shoot him, but at least this way, the deputy had a fighting chance. Plus, there was the possibility that Jameson would be able to help since the gunman was out in the open with Jace.

"I need to listen for footsteps," Jodi said under her breath. "I'll recognize the sound of his steps."

Maybe. But he wasn't sure how she would manage that. Her heart had to be beating a mile a minute right now, and added to that, there was still the occasional gunshot near Hector.

The very direction where they were going.

They crawled, stopping every few feet, and when they reached the first curve in the trail, Gabriel and she got to crouching positions. It still wasn't ideal, but it might give them a fighting chance.

Just ahead were the thickest shrubs. It was also the place where Jodi had been attacked. She knew that, of course, and it was probably why he heard her breath hitch in her throat. Yes, she was a trained security specialist, but she was also the woman who'd nearly died here. No way to erase that from her mind.

"If he gets his hands on me," she said, "kill him."

That was the plan, but Gabriel preferred to do the killing before this monster touched her.

They inched their way up the trail, and Gabriel heard another sound. One that caused him to curse. Not footsteps. Not gunshots. But it was something he instantly recognized.

A rattler.

Hell. They didn't need this now.

It wasn't unusual for rattlesnakes to be out among all the underbrush, but Gabriel figured it could be something that their attacker had planted. Something to get them moving so fast that it'd be easier to kill them.

"Freeze," Gabriel whispered to her.

In the darkness it was going to be pretty much impossible to see the snake, so he followed the sound of it. It was definitely agitated because the rattler was going practically nonstop. A warning to get them to back off. Gabriel wished they could do just that, but instead they had to crouch there and wait it out. That was the plan anyway.

But it didn't happen.

There was some movement to their left. Definitely footsteps this time, and Gabriel got just a glimpse of a hand that reached out from the shrub. The moonlight was just at the right angle for it to glint off the shiny blade.

As the knife plunged right into Jodi.

Chapter Sixteen

The pain shot through Jodi's shoulder. Familiar pain. It brought all the memories crashing back. The nightmare.

He was killing her again.

And she felt the warm blood start to slip down her back.

She took her own knife from her mouth and slashed it at him. Jodi thought maybe she connected with some part of him, but she couldn't tell for sure. That's because he was in the bushes, and she couldn't see him. However, she could see his knife, and he sliced it at her again. She ducked out of the way, barely in time.

If the rattler was still there, it had stopped making that god-awful sound. That was something at least, but it was also possible that it had been a recording. Her attacker probably wouldn't have wanted to risk being bitten by one of his "pets."

From the corner of her eye, she could see Gabriel.

He lunged toward her, taking aim at her attacker, but he didn't get a chance to shoot. That's because the man latched onto her hair and dragged her into the shrubs with him. Gabriel wouldn't have risked shooting because he could have hit her.

She felt another cut from the knife. This time on her arm, and he knocked her blade from her hand. More pain came. Not just from her physical wounds but because once again she was that nineteen-year-old girl. The one who this monster—or maybe the monster who'd hired him—had put in a shallow grave.

For a moment the fear froze her, but then she heard the shot. Heard Gabriel curse, too. And Jace shouted for him to watch out. The gunman who had Jace was no doubt on the trail, too, and he was trying to gun down Gabriel. Or else just keep him occupied while this goon stabbed her. Either way, that got her unfrozen, and Jodi remembered her training.

He still had hold of her hair. The knife, too, but she got to her feet, bashing her head into his chin. That stopped the next blow, but he made a feral sound and took another swing at her.

"Jodi!" Gabriel called out, and she heard him scramble toward her. Heard another shot fired, too. She only prayed they'd get out of this alive, but that might not happen if she didn't stop the knife.

Gabriel pushed through the shrubs, and she got just a glimpse of him before her attacker dragged her to her feet with her back against his chest. Like Jace, she was now a human shield. And she was bleeding. She could feel at least two stab wounds, but it was as if he'd cut her many more times.

Just like that night.

Her attacker motioned for Gabriel to drop his gun, and he put the tip of her knife right at her carotid artery. One jab of the blade, and she'd bleed out in no time at all.

"Let her go," Gabriel tried. "No way can you get out of here alive."

The man's silence let them know he didn't agree with that. For a good reason. He had at least one healthy gunman and two hostages, Jace and her. That would get not only Gabriel but the deputies and Jameson to back off.

He started backing up, dragging her with him. The brushes scraped at her hands. Probably at him, too, but he didn't react. He was solely focused on getting her away from Gabriel. No doubt so he could finish her off.

This wasn't a hired thug. That feral sound he'd made had dripped with emotion. And she doubted it was a coincidence that he'd yet to say anything to them. This wasn't some hired gun. This was the *one*.

She heard it then. The sound that had been in her head for nearly ten years. His footsteps. Yes. They were identical to the ones that night. When he'd been dragging her nearly lifeless body into these very shrubs.

But who was it?

He was wearing a ski mask, so she couldn't see his face even if he would have allowed her to turn around. All of their suspects had similar builds, and she couldn't assume that Hector had truly been hurt. No. All of that could have been faked to bring them to this point.

Jodi let everything inside her go still. Just as Hector had taught her to do, and she gathered her energy. Her focus. And she pinpointed into the only weapon she had readily available to her.

Her own body.

It was a risk, but everything, and nothing, would be at this point. So, she made eye contact with Gabriel to try to give him some kind of heads-up that she was about to make her move. Whether he noticed her look or not she didn't know because he was volleying glances between her attacker and the approaching gunman.

Jodi dropped, her weight dragging her attacker down with her, and in the same motion she rammed her elbow into his ribs. He staggered back, letting go of her and dropping the knife, but she soon realized the only reason he did that was so he could draw a gun and take aim.

He fired at Gabriel.

Thankfully, Gabriel must have realized what was

happening because he was already moving to the side before the man pulled the trigger. The shot blasted into the ground.

Jodi fumbled around, looking for a knife or gun, but the man latched onto her again. He bashed the gun against her wounded shoulder, causing the pain to shoot through her. It was blinding and robbed her of her breath for a few precious seconds. Seconds that he used to drag her in front of him again. But Jodi did some grabbing of her own.

She caught on to the ski mask, dragging it from his face.

And she finally knew who wanted her dead.

Russell.

Even with only the watery moonlight, she saw him smile. A sickening smile that revealed the monster beneath. He'd been the bogeyman all this time.

"Why?" she managed to asked.

"You were a mistake," he said, surprising her with his answer. "I was mad, high and thinking like an idiot when I came here and saw you leave Gabriel's house. I lost my temper."

"You did all of that because you lost your temper?" she repeated, and Jodi didn't bother to take out the sarcasm. Nor the rage that was bubbling up inside her. "You stabbed me and tried to bury me."

"Like I said, it was a mistake. But your mistake was remembering after all this time. I couldn't risk my wife finding out. I'd lose everything."

It twisted at her to hear that. It notched up the anger inside her, too. This sick excuse for a man was ready to murder heaven knew how many people to cover up his crimes.

Gabriel didn't move, but she could tell he was trying to figure out what to do. Once again, he couldn't risk shooting the man, so, like Jodi, he just had to wait and hope for some kind of opportunity.

"A lot of people are dead because of you," Gabriel said, his voice low and dangerous. "Why did you kill my parents?"

"I didn't," he said without hesitation. "They were already dead when I went to their house looking for Jodi. The blood was fresh, as if they'd just been killed. I figured the person who did that to them could still be around, so I ran out. I saw the knife in the yard, picked it up and then spotted Jodi at your house. I waited for her on the trail."

She wasn't sure about the timing of that. Jodi had always assumed that the Becketts had been murdered during a twenty minute or so window when she'd been at Gabriel's. But she'd thought that because of when Ivy had called Gabriel after discovering the bodies. Maybe, though, Ivy hadn't found her parents until minutes after they'd been killed. That would have given Russell time to find the knife, come after her and put her in that grave before Gabriel even started running up the trail to his parents' house.

Of course, Russell might be lying, too.

"That's when I lost my temper," Russell went on. "When I saw her on the trail. I figured she'd just left your bed."

It wouldn't do any good to say that she hadn't done it, that Gabriel had rejected her that night. Even if Russell believed her, it wouldn't change anything that'd happened.

"Is Hector dead?" she asked.

"Maybe. If he's not, he should stay away from me because I'd have to kill him, too."

So, Hector hadn't been a part of this. That was something at least, though it might be too late for Jace and Hector.

"I'm tired of talking now," Russell said, dragging her even deeper into the shrubs just as he'd done ten years ago. "Jodi, I'm thinking you aren't going to cheat death this time—"

"Your wife is suspicious of you," Gabriel interrupted.

That stopped Russell in his tracks. Not Gabriel, though. He moved slightly to the right, and since he still had his gun in his hand, maybe he'd get in a position to shoot. Since the original attack, everything in her life had centered on killing the man who'd done those horrible things to her. But now, she just wanted him dead or at least locked up.

"What are you talking about?" Russell snapped.

"Your wife went to see August earlier today."

Judging from the way Russell's arm tightened, he hadn't known that. "What did that SOB tell her?"

"That he thought you were the one trying to kill Jodi and me."

Russell made another of those vicious sounds. "I'll kill him for doing that. He had no right. That fool has been interfering from day one, always digging, always sticking his nose where it doesn't belong."

"Ironic that you'd mention *rights* when you had a cop murdered so you could set up Hector. Billy and Mara, too. Plus, you might have let an innocent man spend a decade in jail for murders that he didn't commit. I'm guessing you and Mara were having an affair, and that's why she was so willing to help you." Gabriel paused, moved again. "By the way, your wife talked to August about your affair with Mara."

That was a lie, of course, but she understood why Gabriel had said it. It was to make Russell believe that this was all for nothing, that his marriage was going to fall apart after all. That way, he might let them go, so they could get an ambulance out for Jace, Hector and her.

"I'll fix things with Tracy when I'm finished here," Russell mumbled. He was getting more agitated with each passing second. "She's not like Jodi. She's loyal to me."

Jodi could have told him that she hadn't been loyal because they'd dated only a short period of time. It certainly hadn't been serious. Couldn't have been. Because she'd been in love with Gabriel.

Still was.

Too bad it was a tough time to remember that. Because it was also a reminder at how much she had at stake. She couldn't lose him.

She braced herself for Russell to shoot her. And there was a shot. It just hadn't come from him. It had come from the direction of Gabriel's house.

"It's me," Jameson called out. "We've got both gunmen in custody and an ambulance on the way for Hector and Jace. Where's Russell?"

Apparently, one or both the gunmen had decided to rat out their boss. So much for loyalty. Of course, if they were like the others Russell had hired, they were common thugs.

Thugs who could have easily killed them.

"Russell's here," Gabriel answered. "He's holding Jodi at gunpoint."

Before Gabriel had even finished what he was saying, Russell fired, the shot so loud that it blasted through her head. She couldn't hear, but Jodi could certainly feel, and she knew Russell was getting ready to run.

She dropped down before he could do that and grabbed the knife.

Jodi didn't have time to get back up and stab him in the heart, so she just slashed the blade at him, the knife gouging into his stomach.

Russell cursed at her, calling her a vile name, and he backhanded her with the gun. Again, the pain came and put her right back on her knees. Russell took advantage of that. He shoved her at Gabriel.

Gabriel and she collided, both of them falling to the ground.

Russell fired another shot and took off running. Jodi got up to go after him. But she stopped.

Because she saw the blood on Gabriel's chest.

Chapter Seventeen

Gabriel wished he had something to punch—hard. Preferably Russell. That might rid him of some of this lethal energy that was bubbling up inside him.

The pain didn't help with that energy, either. This was his first gunshot wound, and it thankfully hadn't been life-threatening. Russell's bullet had been a through and through into Gabriel's shoulder, but even after some meds, it was throbbing like an abscessed tooth. However, his pain was nothing compared to what he was feeling about Jodi.

Gabriel had refused to leave her side not only for the ambulance ride but while they were both getting examined and stitched up at the hospital. His staying close to her was partially because he was just plain worried about her.

But it was also because her would-be killer was still at large.

Somehow, Russell had managed to escape. Probably because he had a car stashed near the ranch, and he'd no doubt fled while Jameson was concerned with keeping Jace alive. The deputy and Hector were both going to be okay, but their injuries were more serious than Jodi's and his.

Of course, nothing was more serious to Gabriel than seeing the blood all over her. Hell. It was like that night all over again. He'd saved her then, but the cost of that attack had been sky-high, and he wasn't sure how long it would take Jodi to recover a second time. The images of this attack would now be piled on top of the nightmarish memories she already had.

Despite all the blood, Jodi had gotten lucky, too. There was a cut on her upper arm. Another near her left wrist. The doctor had taken off her T-shirt while he'd examined her, so Gabriel had no trouble seeing each wound. The camisole she'd had on beneath her shirt had blood on it, as well.

He wanted to punch something again, and that feeling got worse with every new bruise, cut and scrape he saw on her silky skin.

Jameson stepped into the treatment room, glancing at both of them and shaking his head. "I hope you know how to get bloodstains out of clothes."

It was a really bad joke, and Gabriel scowled at him. Jameson, however, went to Jodi and brushed a kiss on her forehead. She flinched a little, but that was possibly because she was reacting to the stitches that the nurse was just finishing applying to her wounds.

"Please tell me you caught Russell," she said.

"Not yet. But SAPD has officers at his house to protect his wife and baby. I had a Ranger go to August's place just in case, too."

Good idea. Russell had been pretty riled about his wife going to see August, and he might want to find out what the woman had told him. Of course, that was all water under the bridge now. They knew Russell was a killer, and soon his wife would know that, as well.

"I put two deputies at the hospital doors," Jameson went on, and he looked at Jodi's empty hip holster. Gabriel had managed to hold on to his own gun, but Jodi had lost hers in the scuffle. Jameson took out his backup from the slide holster in his jeans and gave it to her. "Just in case."

That put some alarm back in Jodi's eyes. Not that she'd exactly looked calm and serene before his comment, but this was a reminder that Russell could come charging in there and try to kill them. According to the hired guns Jameson had rounded up, there wasn't anybody else on Russell's dirty payroll, but Gabriel had seen the sick hatred in Russell's eyes.

If there was any humanly way he could get to Jodi, he would.

That's why Gabriel was thankful his brother had given her the gun. Now, he had to pray she didn't need it.

Gabriel stood from the table and reached for

his shirt to put it back on. Before he could do that, though, Jameson snatched it away.

"No," Jameson said, "you're not going after Russell."

Since that's exactly what Gabriel had been planning to do, he couldn't deny it, but he could pull rank on a younger brother. He wasn't so sure, though, that he could do that with Jodi.

"You're not going after Russell," she echoed. "Not without me anyway." She stood, too, reaching for her shirt. Wincing and grunting in pain, she started to put it on.

"You're not leaving this hospital," Gabriel warned her.

"And neither are you." Jodi's chin came up, and he could have sworn she was fighting back a smile. Maybe because she'd just one-upped him. He didn't want her out there, so that meant he was staying put, too.

Gabriel went to her with the hopes of convincing her to stay seated. She did but only because he hovered over her and kissed her. He had intended for it to be just a peck, but it felt so good that he lingered a few seconds.

God, he could have lost her.

"I'll see if your rooms are ready," the nurse said, standing. She was fighting back a smile, as well. "And no, it won't do any good to tell Dr. Holliwell that you don't want to stay. He's already said he's keeping both of you for the night."

Yeah, that was an argument he didn't even want to try to win with the doc. Dr. Holliwell wanted Jodi in the hospital in case her injuries were worse than the original diagnosis, and Gabriel didn't want her alone. That meant both Gabriel and she were staying.

"I'll see if there are any updates," Jameson said. "You two look like you could use some alone time."

Gabriel gave him another scowl, but he did want some time with Jodi. There were things he had to tell her.

"I'm so sorry," he started. "I should have stopped this—"

She caught on to his neck, pulling him down to her, and kissed him. It hurt. Mainly because it tweaked the muscles in his throbbing shoulder. But he didn't care. Kissing her was worth the pain.

"I'm the one who should be saying I'm sorry," she insisted. "Russell was on the trail because he thought I would remember that he was the one who'd attacked me."

This called for another kiss to shut her up, but Gabriel got in something else he wanted to say first. "Neither one of us made Russell a killer. He did that all by himself."

And they'd both be cleaning up Russell's mess for a long, long time.

Now, he kissed her, and it wasn't to hush her. It

was because he needed it. Judging from the sound she made in her throat, she needed it, as well. The kiss might have gone on a lot longer if his phone hadn't buzzed. Since it could be about Russell, he stepped back to take the call.

"It's August," he told her after seeing the name on the screen.

He considered letting it go to voice mail, but since August was in possible danger, he hit Answer and put it on speaker.

"Is it true?" August practically yelled. "Is that idiot Russell after me?"

"He could be. I told him that his wife had visited you."

August cursed him. And Gabriel let him go on for a while. In hindsight he probably should have figured out a different way to get Russell to confess to using Mara and then murdering her, but considering everything else that had been going on, it was the best he could do.

"I want you to stay in your house with the Rangers," Gabriel told him. "If Russell shows up, have the Rangers call me."

"Hell, no, I won't. I'll kill him on sight. And in the meantime, you'll get my brother out of jail. This proves he didn't—"

"Russell said he didn't kill my parents."

"And you believed him?" August howled.

"Yeah, I did. Because he didn't deny murdering

Mara. Didn't deny attacking Jodi, either." Gabriel had to pause and gather his breath. It was hard to think of just how close Russell had come to ending her life—again. "If he had killed them, I believe Russell would have taken great pleasure in letting me know."

Jodi nodded in agreement. "It would have made things easier, for me anyway, if Russell had committed all the murders."

Yes, because it would mean her father was innocent. And with Russell's confession, Travis was clear of Jodi's attack. But clearing his name didn't extend to the deaths of Gabriel's parents. No. There wasn't enough evidence to overturn his conviction. However, it was something Gabriel would take a closer look at. Jodi would no doubt do the same.

Jodi took hold of his hand, gave it a gentle squeeze. Considering it was such a small gesture, it had a big effect. It didn't rid him of the ache in his heart, but it sure as heck helped.

"Don't think I'm just going to drop this," August went on. "As soon as you catch Russell, I'm finding a judge who'll set Travis free." With that, he ended the call.

"That won't happen," Gabriel assured Jodi.

She nodded. "I agree. If Russell had killed them, he would have said so." She paused. "But at least now I know my father wasn't the one who attacked me."

In all the chaos, Gabriel had forgotten just how

important that was to her. Good. It might help with
the nightmares and panic attacks. But she certainly
wasn't panicking now.

She slipped right into his arms.

"I'm in love with you, you know," she said.

No. He hadn't known. And it left him speechless.
Not the best time for that because she was clearly
waiting for him to respond. Before he could get his
mouth working, though, the nurse stepped in.

"Are you up to seeing Hector March?" The nurse
directed her question to Jodi. "He's asking for you."

Gabriel wasn't sure it was a good idea, especially
since Hector might verbally blast Jodi again for not
sticking up for him, but he didn't stop her when she
started to follow the nurse. Gabriel did go with her,
though. For one thing, because she didn't look steady
on her feet. For another, he didn't want her alone.

The hospital wasn't that large by anyone's stan-
dards, and it took them less than a minute to make
it to the room where Hector was recovering. Unlike
Jodi and him, Hector had required some surgery.
Ditto for Jace, but both had come out of it just fine.
Physically fine anyway.

The moment Jodi and Gabriel stepped into the
room, Hector tried to sit up, but the nurse motioned
for him to lie back down. He didn't listen. Instead,
he winced and grunted until he got into the position
he wanted. Probably so he'd be able to face them
head-on.

Hector's mouth tightened when he looked at Jodi. "I would ask if you're okay, but I can see you're not." His attention lingered on the bloodstains on her shirt. "He knifed you?"

She nodded. "This time, though, he didn't hit any vital organs, and I did manage to cut him." Jodi tipped her head to the fresh bandage on his leg and chest. "How about you? Are you okay?"

"I'll be fine in no time. Just a few broken ribs."

"And two gunshot wounds," Jodi added. "The doctor mentioned it when he was examining Gabriel and me."

"Flesh wounds. I'll be back at work tomorrow."

"In a week if you're lucky," the nurse corrected, and she stepped out.

Gabriel was betting Hector wasn't going to stay in that bed for a week. A night maybe, until the effects of the anesthesia wore off.

"It can't be easy for you to be here," Hector went on, and it surprised Gabriel that the man wasn't speaking to Jodi but to him. "You're probably blaming yourself for what happened to Jodi. I know I sure as hell am."

Jodi frowned. "It wasn't your fault." She looked at Gabriel and repeated it before she went to Hector and slid her hand over his.

Hector stared at her, clearly surprised. Maybe because Jodi wasn't the touching type. Ironic that she could manage to do it now when she'd just weathered another attack.

"Thank you for everything you did for me," she said.

Hector's stare continued. "But?"

Jodi drew in a long breath. "But I can't work for you any longer. And no, it doesn't have anything to do with what went on tonight."

"It has to do with Gabriel." Hector huffed, groaned softly and then scrubbed his hand over his face. "I'm guessing he's the reason I no longer see the panic in your eyes?"

She nodded. "He's the reason for a lot of things."

That got him a quick glare from Hector. Then, a nod. Hector and he would probably never be friendly to each other, but they could agree on one thing. They wanted what was best for Jodi. Because they both cared deeply for her.

"You're not going to become a cop, are you?" Hector asked, and it sounded as if he was only partially joking. Partially disgusted with the thought of that, too.

"No, but maybe a PI. That way, I can put all the training you gave me to good use. I can still help people. Protect them, maybe. I could even set up an office right here in Blue River."

So, she was staying. Or least thinking of staying. Even though it wasn't a sure thing, it felt as if someone had lifted a weight off his shoulders.

Hector stayed quiet a moment while he continued to study Jodi's face. "Is this goodbye then?"

"Yes," she answered after a long pause. "Thanks again, Hector." She leaned down, dropped a kiss on his forehead.

Gabriel hated the punch of jealousy that went through him. Especially since it was obvious that Jodi didn't have any romantic feelings for her former boss, but Gabriel was just feeling possessive at the moment. That probably had something to do with what she'd said to him.

I'm in love with you, you know.

He was definitely still reeling from that. Because, no, he hadn't known.

The moment they were back in the hall, Gabriel eased her into his arms. He'd intended it to be just a hug since he figured she needed a little TLC after that chat. Of course, nothing ever stayed just a simple hug with them, so when she looked up at him, Gabriel kissed her. He would have also brought up that "I'm in love with you" if he hadn't heard the footsteps heading their way. He automatically stepped in front of Jodi and drew his gun.

But again, it was only Jameson.

However, unlike earlier when Jameson had come into the treatment room, his brother was now smiling. "The Rangers found Russell."

Gabriel still had his arm around Jodi, and he felt

her practically sag against him in relief. "Where was he?" she asked.

"Not far from the ranch. He was on one of the old trails. He's dead," Jameson added a heartbeat later.

Gabriel's mind started to whirl with all sorts of bad scenarios—like a shoot-out where more law enforcement officers had been hurt, or worse. "Did Russell kill anyone else?"

Jameson shook his head. "He didn't get the chance. He bled out while sitting in his car. A knife wound to the stomach. Your doing?" he asked Gabriel.

"No. Jodi's."

So, she'd killed Russell after all.

Gabriel looked down at her to see how she was handling that. No tears. And she seemed a little stronger than she had been a couple of seconds earlier. Relieved, too.

"Good," she whispered.

Yeah, it was. Not only because they didn't have to worry about Russell coming after them, but because he also couldn't try to kill his wife or August. Of course, his wife's troubles were just beginning, because she'd have to live with the aftermath of what her husband had done.

"Are you okay?" Jameson asked her, but he waved it off. "Of course, you are. You're in good hands." He smiled, no doubt noticing that Gabriel and she were practically wrapped around each other, and he strolled off.

"Are you really okay?" Gabriel repeated to her.

She took a moment, as if trying to figure out how to answer him, and then nodded. "For years, I've dreamed about this happening. About getting back at my attacker. But now that I've managed it, it no longer seems important. *This* is what's important."

Gabriel hoped that she was talking about him. "Earlier you said you were in love with me."

She stared at him, maybe trying to figure out how he felt about that and how he felt about her. But Gabriel didn't want there to be any question in her mind.

"Right back at you," he said. He even managed a smile before he kissed her. And because he figured she needed the words as well, Gabriel added, "I'm in love with you, too."

Now, she smiled. Kissed him and slid as close to him as their injuries would allow.

She'd been right. This was what was important. And Gabriel now had everything he wanted right in his arms.

* * * * *

Look for the next book in USA TODAY
bestselling author Delores Fossen's
BLUE RIVER RANCH *miniseries,*
available next month.

And don't miss the most recent books
in her long-running series,
THE LAWMEN OF SILVER CREEK RANCH:

LANDON
HOLDEN
DRURY
LUCAS

*Sheriff Flint Cahill can and will endure elements
far worse than the coming winter storm to hunt
down Maggie Thompson and her abductor.*

Read on for a sneak preview of
COWBOY'S LEGACY,
A CAHILL RANCH NOVEL *from*
New York Times *bestselling author*
B.J. Daniels!

SHE WAS IN so fast that she didn't have a chance to scream. The icy cold water stole her breath away. Her eyes flew open as she hit. Because of the way she fell, she had no sense of up or down for a few moments.

Panicked, she flailed in the water until a light flickered above her. She tried to swim toward it, but something was holding her down. The harder she fought, the more it seemed to push her deeper and deeper, the light fading.

Her lungs burned. She had to breathe. The dim light wavered above her through the rippling water. She clawed at it as her breath gave out. She could see the surface just inches above her. Air! She needed oxygen. Now!

The rippling water distorted the face that suddenly appeared above her. The mouth twisted in a grotesque smile. She screamed, only to have her throat fill with the putrid dark water. She choked, sucking in even more water. She was drowning, and the person who'd done this to her was watching her die and smiling.

Maggie Thompson shot upright in bed, gasping for air and swinging her arms frantically toward the faint light coming through the window. Panic had her perspiration-soaked nightgown sticking to her skin. Trembling, she clutched the bedcovers as she gasped for breath.

The nightmare had been so real this time that she thought she was going to drown before she could come out of it. Her chest ached, her throat feeling raw as tears burned her eyes. It had been too real. She couldn't shake the feeling that she'd almost died this time. Next time...

She snapped on the bedside lamp to chase away the dark shadows hunkered in the corners of the room. If only Flint had been here instead of on an all-night stakeout. She needed Sheriff Flint Cahill's strong arms around her. Not that he stayed most nights. They hadn't been intimate that long.

Often, he had to work or was called out in the middle of the night. He'd asked her to move in with him months ago, but she'd declined. He'd asked her after one of his ex-wife's nasty tricks. Maggie hadn't wanted to make a decision like that based on Flint's ex.

While his ex hadn't done anything in months to keep them apart, Maggie couldn't rest easy. Flint was hoping Celeste had grown tired of her tricks. Maggie wasn't that naive. Celeste Duma was one of those women who played on every man's weakness to get what she wanted—and she wanted not just the rich, powerful man she'd left Flint for. She wanted to keep her ex on the string, as well.

Maggie's breathing slowed a little. She pulled the covers up to her chin, still shivering, but she didn't turn off the light. Sleep was out of the question for a while. She told herself that she wasn't going to let Celeste scare her. She wasn't going to give the woman the satisfaction.

Unfortunately, it was just bravado. Flint's ex was obsessed with him. Obsessed with keeping them apart. And since the woman had nothing else to do...

As the images of the nightmare faded, she reminded herself that the dream made no sense. It never had. She was a good swimmer. Loved water. Had never nearly drowned. Nor had anyone ever tried to drown her.

Shuddering, she thought of the face she'd seen through the rippling water. Not Celeste's. More like a Halloween mask. A distorted smiling face, neither male nor female. Just the memory sent her heart racing again.

What bothered her most was that dream kept reoccurring. After the first time, she'd mentioned it to her friend Belle Delaney.

"A drowning dream?" Belle had asked with the

arch of her eyebrow. "Do you feel that in waking life you're being 'sucked into' something you'd rather not be a part of?"

Maggie had groaned inwardly. Belle had never kept it a secret that she thought Maggie was making a mistake when it came to Flint. Too much baggage, she always said of the sheriff. His "baggage" came in the shape of his spoiled, probably psychopathic, petite, green-eyed, blonde ex.

"I have my own skeletons." Maggie had laughed, although she'd never shared her past—even with Belle—before moving to Gilt Edge, Montana, and opening her beauty shop, Just Hair. She feared it was her own baggage that scared her the most.

"If you're holding anything back," Belle had said, eyeing her closely, "you need to let it out. Men hate surprises after they tie the knot."

"Guess I don't have to worry about that because Flint hasn't said anything about marriage." But she knew Belle was right. She'd even come close to telling him several times about her past. Something had always stopped her. The truth was, she feared if he found out her reasons for coming to Gilt Edge he wouldn't want her anymore.

"The dream isn't about Flint," she'd argued that day with Belle, but she couldn't shake the feeling that it was a warning.

"Well, from what I know about dreams," Belle had said, "if in the dream you survive the drowning, it means that a waking relationship will ultimately survive the turmoil. At least, that is one interpretation. But I'd say the nightmare definitely indicates that you are going into unknown waters and something is making you leery of where you're headed." She'd cocked an eyebrow at her. "If you have the dream again, I'd suggest that you ask yourself what it is you're so afraid of."

"I'm sure it's just about his ex, Celeste," she'd lied. Or was she afraid that she wasn't good enough for Flint—just as his ex had warned her. Just as she feared in her heart.

THE WIND LAY over the tall dried grass and kicked up dust as Sheriff Flint Cahill stood on the hillside. He shoved his Stetson down on his head of thick dark hair, squinting in the distance at the clouds to the west. Sure as the devil, it was going to snow before the day was out.

In the distance, he could see a large star made out of red and green lights on the side of a barn, a reminder that Christmas was coming. Flint thought he might even get a tree this year, go up in the mountains and cut it himself. He hadn't had a tree at Christmas in years. Not since...

At the sound of a pickup horn, he turned, shielding his eyes from the low winter sun. He could smell snow in the air, feel it deep in his bones. This storm was going to dump a good foot on them, according to the latest news. They were going to have a white Christmas.

Most years he wasn't ready for the holiday season any more than he was ready for a snow that wouldn't melt until spring. But this year was different. He felt energized. This was the year his life would change. He thought of the small velvet box in his jacket pocket. He'd been carrying it around for months. Just the thought of it made him smile to himself. He was in love and he was finally going to do something about it.

The pickup rumbled to a stop a few yards from him. He took a deep breath of the mountain air and, telling himself he was ready for whatever Mother Nature wanted to throw at him, he headed for the truck.

"Are you all right?" his sister asked as he slid into the passenger seat. In the cab out of the wind, it was nice and warm. He rubbed his bare hands together, wishing he hadn't forgotten his gloves earlier. But when he'd headed out, he'd had too much on his mind. He still did.

Lillie looked out at the dull brown of the landscape and the chain-link fence that surrounded the missile silo. "What were you doing out here?"

He chuckled. "Looking for aliens. What else?" This was the spot that their father swore aliens hadn't just landed on one night back in 1967. Nope, according to Ely Cahill, the aliens had abducted him, taken him aboard their spaceship and done experiments on him. Not that anyone believed it in the county. Everyone just assumed that Ely had a screw loose. Or two.

It didn't help that their father spent most of the year up in the mountains as a recluse trapping and panning for gold.

"Aliens. Funny," Lillie said, making a face at him.

He smiled over at her. "Actually, I was on an all-night stakeout. The cattle rustlers didn't show up." He shrugged.

She glanced around. "Where's your patrol SUV?"

"Axle deep in a muddy creek back toward Grass Range. I'll have to get it pulled out. After I called you, I started walking and I ended up here. Wish I'd grabbed my gloves, though."

"You're scaring me," she said, studying him openly. "You're starting to act like Dad."

He laughed at that, wondering how far from the truth it was. "At least I didn't see any aliens near the missile silo."

She groaned. Being the butt of jokes in the county because of their father got old for all of them.

Flint glanced at the fenced-in area. There was nothing visible behind the chain link but tumbleweeds. He turned back to her. "I didn't pull you away from anything important, I hope? Since you were close by, I thought you wouldn't mind giving me a ride. I've had enough walking for one day. Or thinking, for that matter."

She shook her head. "What's going on, Flint?"

He looked out at the country that ran to the mountains. Cahill Ranch. His grandfather had started it, his father had worked it and now two of his brothers ran the cattle part of it to keep the place going while he and his sister, Lillie, and brother Darby had taken other paths. Not to mention their oldest brother, Tucker, who'd struck out at seventeen and hadn't been seen or heard from since.

Flint had been scared after his marriage and divorce. But Maggie was nothing like Celeste, who was small, blonde, green-eyed and crazy. Maggie was tall with big brown eyes and long auburn hair. His heart beat faster at the thought of her smile, at her laugh.

"I'm going to ask Maggie to marry me," Flint said and nodded as if reassuring himself.

When Lillie didn't reply, he glanced over at her. It wasn't like her not to have something to say. "Well?"

"What has taken you so long?"

He sighed. "Well, you know after Celeste…"

"Say no more," his sister said, raising a hand to stop him. "Anyone would be gun-shy after being married to her."

"I'm hoping she won't be a problem."

Lillie laughed. "Short of killing your ex-wife, she is always going to be a problem. You just have to decide if you're going to let her run your life. Or if you're going to live it—in spite of her."

So easy for her to say. He smiled, though. "You're right. Anyway, Maggie and I have been dating for a while now and there haven't been any...incidents in months."

Lillie shook her head. "You know Celeste was the one who vandalized Maggie's beauty shop—just as you know she started that fire at Maggie's house."

"Too bad there wasn't any proof so I could have arrested her. But since there wasn't and no one was hurt and it was months ago..."

"I'd love to see Celeste behind bars, though I think prison is too good for her. I can understand why you would be worried about what she will do next. She's psychopathic."

He feared that that maybe was close to the case. "Do you want to see the ring?" He knew she did, so he fished it out of his pocket. He'd been carrying it around for quite a while now. Getting up his courage? He knew what was holding him back. Celeste. He couldn't be sure how she would take it—or what she might do. His ex-wife seemed determined that he and Maggie shouldn't be together, even though she was apparently happily married to local wealthy businessman Wayne Duma.

Handing his sister the small black velvet box, he waited as she slowly opened it.

A small gasp escaped her lips. "It's beautiful. *Really* beautiful." She shot him a look. "I thought sheriffs didn't make much money?"

"I've been saving for a long while now. Unlike my sister, I live pretty simply."

She laughed. "Simply? Prisoners have more in their cells than you do. You aren't thinking of living in that small house of yours after you're married, are you?"

"For a while. It's not that bad. Not all of us have huge new houses like you and Trask."

"We need the room for all the kids we're going to have," she said. "But it is wonderful, isn't it? Trask is determined that I have everything I ever wanted." Her gaze softened as the newlywed thought of her husband.

"I keep thinking of your wedding." There'd been a double wedding, with both Lillie and her twin, Darby, getting married to the loves of their lives only months ago. "It's great to see you and Trask so happy. And Darby and Mariah… I don't think Darby is ever going to come off that cloud he's on."

Lillie smiled. "I'm so happy for him. And I'm happy for you. You know I really like Maggie. So do it. Don't worry about Celeste. Once you're married, there's nothing she can do."

He told himself she was right, and yet in the back of his mind, he feared that his ex-wife would do something to ruin it—just as she had done to some of his dates with Maggie.

"I don't understand Celeste," Lillie was saying as she shifted into Drive and started toward the small Western town of Gilt Edge. "She's the one who dumped you for Wayne Duma. So what is her problem?"

"I'm worried that she is having second thoughts about her marriage to Duma. Or maybe she's bored and has nothing better to do than concern herself with my life. Maybe she just doesn't want me to be happy."

"Or she is just plain malicious," Lillie said. "If she isn't happy, she doesn't want you to be, either."

A shaft of sunlight came through the cab window, warming him against the chill that came with even talking about Celeste. He leaned back, content as Lillie drove.

He was going to ask Maggie to marry him. He was going to do it this weekend. He'd already made a dinner reservation at the local steak house. He had the ring in his pocket. Now it was just a matter of popping the question and hoping she said yes. If she did… Well, then, this was going to be the best Christmas ever, he thought and smiled.

* * * * *

Don't miss COWBOY'S LEGACY,
available December 2017
wherever HQN Books and
ebooks are sold.

www.Harlequin.com

SPECIAL EXCERPT FROM

⊕ HARLEQUIN®
™

I N T R I G U E

To say Riker County detective Matt Walker and
journalist Maggie Carson have bad blood is an
understatement. But when the last twenty-four hours
of her memory go missing and she gets caught in
someone's crosshairs, the lawman who hates her may be
her only salvation…

Read on for a sneak preview of
FORGOTTEN PIECES
by Tyler Anne Snell.

Everyone worked through grief differently.

Some people started a new hobby; some people threw themselves into the gym.

Others investigated unsolved murders in secret.

"And why, of all people, would you need me here?" Matt asked, cutting through her mental breakdown of him.

Instead of stepping backward, utilizing the large open space of her front porch, she chanced a step forward.

"I found something," she started, straining out any excess enthusiasm that might make her seem coarse. Still, she knew the detective was a keen observer. Which was why his frown was already doubling in on itself before she explained herself.

"I don't want to hear this," he interrupted, his voice like ice. "I'm warning you, Carson."

"And it wouldn't be the first time you've done so," she countered, skipping over the fact he'd said her last name like a teacher getting ready to send her to detention. "But right now I'm telling you I found a lead. A real, honest-to-God lead!"

The detective's frown affected all of his body. It pinched his expression and pulled his posture taut. Through gritted teeth, he rumbled out his thoughts with disdain clear in his words.

"Why do you keep doing this? What gives you the right?" He took a step away from her. That didn't stop Maggie.

"It wasn't an accident," she implored. "I can prove it now."

Matt shook his head. He skipped frustrated and flew right into angry. This time Maggie faltered.

"You have no right digging into this," he growled. "You didn't even know Erin."

"But don't you want to hear what I found?"

Matt made a stop motion with his hands. The jaw she'd been admiring was set. Hard. "I don't want to ever talk to you again. Especially about this." He turned and was off the front porch in one fluid motion. Before he got into his truck he paused. "And next time you call me out here, I won't hesitate to arrest you."

And then he was gone.

Don't miss
FORGOTTEN PIECES
available January 2018 wherever
Harlequin® Intrigue books and ebooks are sold.

EXCLUSIVE
Limited Time Offer

$1.⁰⁰ OFF

New York Times bestselling author
B.J. DANIELS
returns to her captivating *Cahill Ranch*
series with a brand-new tale!

COWBOY'S
LEGACY

Available November 28, 2017.
Pick up your copy today!

H
HQN™

$7.99 U.S./$9.99 CAN.